The Cuckold Chronicles:

13 Humiliation, Hot Wife, and Cuckold Stories

Thomas Handover

CONTENTS

The Cuckold's Revenge:
Tied Up and Forced to Watch

I was flying home from New York city after my job sent me there for a mandatory week long conference. I was scheduled to stay for 7 nights but caught a flight back a night early due to becoming homesick and desperately wanting to see my wife. I was bored and ready to go home. I had three days off now, so I wanted to fly back and enjoy those three days off with my wife inside the comfort of my own home.

My job requires me to travel frequently. At least once a month for a week at minimum. Because of it, my wife and I were slowly growing apart. But despite that, she was still the favorite aspect of my life. I know it saddens her to see me leave but it's for the greater good as I make more money than I deserve – which is more than enough to cover both of us so that she doesn't even have to work at all.

When I am out of town, she stays behind and looks after the house. She has a serious fear of flying and refuses to go with me.

I did not tell my wife I was flying home as I wanted it to be a surprise. I just love seeing her eyes joyfully light up each time I walked through that door and coming home a night earlier would be extra special for her. I really enjoyed surprising her and I knew that this would.

As we landed and exited the plane, I grabbed my luggage and made for the exit. I saw my car sitting in the parking lot exactly as I left it. I got in, paid my ticket and made the 20 minute drive home to our quaint little house tucked away from civilization.

It was already past midnight so I knew my wife would be asleep. When I pulled up, all the lights were off in the house. I immediately killed my headlights so it wouldn't startle or scare her. I wanted to be as quiet as possible and simply wake her up as a surprise. If she saw or heard me coming, it would scare the living daylights out of her.

As quietly as I could, I unlocked and opened the door. As soon as I entered, I could hear a thumping sound coming from the up-stairs. It was nonstop and constant, like wood slapping against a hardwood floor. Tap… tap… tap… tap… tap… tap… That is basically what it sounded like.

I was taken aback by this, not knowing what it was. I knew she was asleep so what could this possibly be I kept thinking to myself.

As I quietly made my way up the stairs and the closer I got to our bedroom door, I began to hear a faint and deep moaning sound coming from the direction of our bedroom.

I absolutely 100 percent refused to believe what it obviously was. As I drew closer and closer, the moaning sound grew louder. Before grabbing the door handle, I stopped to reflect on so many things about life as quickly as I could in my head. And then, I opened it…

What I saw was horrific and life changing. What I saw was simp-ly put: stunning. I saw a completely naked man on top of my wife with her legs hiked high in the air in the guillotine position and he was bouncing away. He was covered in sweat.

I could not believe what I saw. Never in a million years did I ev-er believe my wife of all people would be doing this to me. All I could think about was how many different men had she been with? How long has she been doing this behind my back? How many times has she been with this particular guy? How many times has she fucked this dude or some other random dude in MY bed – the bed that I sleep in?

So many questions were running rapidly through my head.

He kept pounding away as she gripped his back with one hand and slapped the bed with the other – completely consumed by in-tense pleasure that he was giving her.

All I could do was stand there in the doorway and watch – com-pletely and utterly horrified and shocked beyond all belief.

I watched as he leaned up and wrapped his arms around both of his legs. Now on his knees while she was still on her back, he began fucking here once again. The bed was rocking against the walls, which explained the tapping noise I heard upon entering.

She was moaning in intense pleasure as her hands were all over the place. They were like a freaking octopus. They were everywhere. It was as if she could not control herself as the pleasure this man was giving her was completely controlling her mind, emotions and body.

Neither one of them was aware of my presence. In fact, it would take a lot to get them to notice me. I could literally walk right up to them, slap them in the face and scream bloody murder and yet, they probably still wouldn't notice me. Yes, they were that consumed in the mind controlling pleasure they were giving each other. It was as if they were both out of their minds.

I could not see who the guy was as all I could see was a bare, sweaty back and a little ass with a farmer's tan. The guy had black hair but I had no clue as to who he was.

He kept tearing away at my wife's pussy before he finally slowed to a stop. He pulled out, lifted her up, spun her around on her knees and slid his dick in from behind in the doggie style position and began pounding her out from behind.

My wife reached up and gripped the top of the bed's headboard as tightly as she could as it smashed into the wall repeatedly. He was smashing her hard and she was now to the point of screaming.

Neither one of them knew I was here. They did not know that I was standing here watching them. I wondered how my wife would react if I interrupted them. Would she even apologize? Would she even feel bad? Probably not. She was too caught up in the throes of passion to even give three shits whether I caught her or not

A few more minutes passed and the guy pulled out and spun around. That is when I saw who he was. It was a guy named Marty, who my wife worked with. He was also a married man with two kids. My wife and I had gone out with them on several occasions and even went to a few of their house parties together. I never suspected anything between them. They never even gave off a hint. Marty and his wife seemed like they were happily in love and the quintessential couple. Hell, they had me and my wife beaten by not one but many miles.

Knowing it was him was more of a shock than finding out my wife was cheating on me and seeing it live and in person. I simply could not believe he would do this – not only to me – but to his wife and his children as well.

I watched as he laid down on his back and my wife – whose face was registering blankness due to the pleasure he was giving her – crawled on top of him, spread her legs wide, grabbed his dick and positioned it just right, then angled her pussy above his dick before dropping down on it, swallowing his cock whole with her pussy. The strange thing was, I could now see his dick and it was surprisingly small and a hell of a lot smaller than mine. My dick was borderline seven inches and I was not ashamed of it. I was proud. So why in the hell is my wife fucking a guy with a dick that was much smaller than mine? What the hell did he have that I did not have? He was a beta male, very, very scrawny and was very feminine for a man. He was the complete opposite of me. But perhaps that is the kind of dude my wife was secretly into.

At this point, all I could think about was revenge. Revenge on both of them for what they are doing to me. So, I concocted a plan in my mind. I pulled out my cellphone and began to record these two going at it. You could see Marty's face as plain as day as my wife was just hopping up and down on his little dick.

I recorded about ten minutes of their fuck session, then I wanted to follow through with my plan. So as quietly as I could, I left the house and decided to drive over to Marty's house.

I pulled into the driveway and parked. It took a second to really gain a little courage so that I could fully implement my plan: and I did just that. I gained the right amount of courage and stepped out.

The house was dark and quiet but I did not care. I walked up to the door and rung the doorbell. It took a second and the door finally opened. It was Marty's wife, Rebecca.

Rebecca was a very attractive woman whom I would never even think twice of doing anything with – at least before this – as she and

Marty seemed happily in love and beforehand, I would not want to do such a thing to Marty. But now? She was officially open game and it was open season.

Even recently awakened and without make up, she was a dime piece. She seemed surprised and stunned to see me.

"Is everything okay? Do you know what time it is?" she asked me.

I simply shook my head and agreement. I know she could tell by the look on my face that I had bad news to deliver.

"Look, is there any way I can come in and speak with you a moment?" I asked. "It is very, very important and urgent."

She simply replied, "Yes," and opened the door completely, inviting me in.

I entered the house I had been to a million times with my wife. Like I said, we went to a lot of parties here.

We walked to the living room and sat down on the couch beside each other. It took a second as I didn't know what to say or do.

"What's wrong? Is Marty okay? He's supposed to be working!" She said.

So I sat there silent a moment and then replied with all I knew to say, "I don't know how to tell you this, Rebecca, because I am in the same boat as you're about to be. All I can do is show you. But it is graphic and shocking."

She then said, "So show me! If it's that important, I need to see it!"

So I pulled out my phone, turned the volume down a bit, found the very video of Marty fucking my wife and pushed play before handing her the phone.

As soon as she saw it, her eyes widened and her mouth dropped. She was shocked and disturbed. She could not believe what she was seeing, much like I was.

Her hand covered her mouth. Tears began to fall from her eyes. She then forced me to take the phone back as she began to cry tears of deep emotional sadness. All those years together was a waste. A family now ruined.

She was quiet at first. I simply reached over and grabbed her hand, comfortingly.

"12 years… we were together 12 fucking years. I can't believe this." She said. Then she looked at me with sincerity in her eyes and said, "I am truly sorry he did this to you."

I looked her square in the eye and replied, "It's not your fault. We're in this together now." I grabbed her hand tight to let her know that I meant what I said. Then she buried her head into my shoulder and began to weep. She put her arms around me as I did the same, comforting her as best as I could. I grabbed her tight as she grabbed me tight as well.

"If there is anything I can do, please let me know," I said in an encouraging tone. She stayed silent and continued to cry.

Then she leaned up with a new facial display. "I want to pay him back for what he has done to me," she stated.

"How so?" I asked.

"I don't know, but I want to get that bastard back." She replied.

She went silent and finally, I broke that silence by cutting to the chase, saying, "I think you're a very attractive woman."

She smiled, shyly. It took her a second as the tears dried up to say, "And I think you're a very attractive man."

"I know of a way we could make both him and my wife suffer," I said.

Reading my mind, she knew what I was implying. She simply nodded her head with a big smile and said, "My kids leave at 8 in the morning. You can stay here in the guest bedroom if you'd like. He will be home around 9. That's when we can get him."

I gave her a big friendly smile and then leaned in and kissed her. It was a long kiss as well and I could hear her breathing intensifying as I held it. She was enjoying it… and I couldn't wait to fuck her — right in front of her bloody, soon to be ex husand.

And so I went outside, grabbed a spare camera and tripod from my trunk, went back inside and ventured up the stairs into the guest bedroom. I sat my stuff down and slipped into bed and closed my eyes, ready for the big show I was going to put on tomorrow.

I woke up to Rebecca standing before my bed looking hotter than ever. She was dressed as if she was going out and had her face covered in make up (even though she was so gorgeous, she did not need make up). She obviously wanted to torture this man.

She smiled at me and said, "He should be here in thirty minutes. Go ahead and shower and when you get out, I will need you to hide in my closet."

And so I hopped up and jumped in the shower. I went as fast as I could but made sure everything was clean for this beautiful woman who was soon to be a victim of my dick.

I jumped out, dried off and redressed myself. I ran into the hall-way to discover rosebuds leading from down the stairs and into her bedroom. I walked in to see the rose buds leading to her bed where she laid on it looking as sexy as ever.

"Hide in this closet and wait until I give you a cue." She instructed me. "What is the cue?" I asked.

She then winked at me while wearing a smile and said, "Trust me, you'll know."

I saw my camera and tripod up in front of the bed. Then I ran in the nearby closet and shut the door. It was dark and claustrophobic but I knew the end result would be worth it. Shortly after – roughly five minutes or so – I heard the front door open from downstairs.

"Honey…?" The little bitch yelled out. Everything went silent a moment until I heard footsteps coming up the stairs. "You are really outdoing yourself with this one," he said.

The footsteps kept climbing until they finally reached the top. Then he walked up to the door and opened it.

I heard him say, "Wow!" Then I heard her say seductively, "Have a seat!"

I then heard a little commotion but I couldn't pinpoint what the sounds were. He then said, "You know I love surprises." That is when she said, "And I have a big surprise for you…"

Everything went silent and I knew as something inside told me that this was my cue. I opened the door wearing the most sinister look on my face. When I opened it, I immediately saw Marty bound to a chair with her hovering over him. His face dropped and he was speechless. He stared at me with fear, not knowing whether I was going to kill him, beat the living shit out of him or what. His lips began to quiver but they formed no words. Then, she reared back and slapped the hell out of his face. It threw him out of his catatonic state as he looked at her with puppy dog eyes.

"Honey, what is going on?" He asked fearfully.

"You know what the fuck is going on. I know what the fuck you've been doing and who you've been fucking. And now, you're going to watch me fuck a real man." She said.

He was busted! His eyes lit up. Marty was someone I could clearly destroy in a fight and he knew that. So there was nothing more he could do but sit and watch. And me? I was going to thoroughly enjoy this one.

I walked up to his wife and wrapped my arms around her. Then I shoved my tongue into her mouth and began making out with her as loudly and as obnoxiously as I could.

"Please," he pleaded, "isn't there some other way? Isn't there something we can work out? Honey, think of the children!"

I broke away from his gorgeous wife and grabbed his face as firmly as I could and told him to shut the fuck up and watch. Like the little bitch that he was, he did just that.

I picked up where I left off making out with his wife. Our hands began feeling all over one another. Then I pulled her shirt off to see an amazing body with tits that were just right and six pack abs. Her skin was dark and tan. But not overly dark, just the right amount of shade you like seeing on a woman's skin.

I began to lick her neck and then her boobs and then her abdomen. I leaned up and unstrapped her bra as her tits just popped out at me. By now, she had removed my shirt and was feeling all over my chest and abs.

I grabbed her tits, squeezing them as tightly as I could. Then I began to suck on them as if they were the last pair of tits I would ever suck on. I could feel her body tensing up and her breathing picking up. She was code red horny and just aching for my dick to be placed inside of her… and it would be soon.

I just could not get enough of her tits. My wife's tits were no where near as perfect as Rebecca's. I didn't want to give them up but knew I had to move on although I would be coming back to them soon.

I reached down and slid my hands into her pants, grabbing her thick plump ass. Then I unbuttoned her jeans and pulled them off to see that she wasn't wearing any panties. Her little pussy was already moist and you could not tell that she had kids. Her pussy was perfect and there were no stretch marks anywhere on her amazing body.

I spun her around to face her little bitch ass husband and from behind her, I reached around and began playing with her pussy. Marty was in borderline tears. She began to grind my hand and moan as I kept playing with it. My fingers were covered in her pussy juice as she was oozing that badly.

I was taunting him and it felt amazing. I then dropped down and began to grab her ass. I licked both cheeks as I kept squeezing them like they were a stress reliever.

I then stood up, pulled my pants and underwear down, then saw her face light up as she saw my rock hard dick. I grabbed her by the head and forced her down on her knees. I looked over at her husband who had his eyes closed.

"Open those eyes, you little bitch!" I commanded.

He slowly opened them just in time to see his wife swallowing my dick. It felt so great! Her lips and mouth were perfect. She began to suck on my dick slowly. It was already rock hard and she was doing her best to make sure that it stayed that way.

She grabbed it with one hand and proceeded to both jerk it and suck it at the same time. I could feel my body weakening from the pleasure.

With her other hand, she gently began to rub my balls as she continued to suck and jerk my cock. I was groaning with peeking over at her husband who look mentally defeated. But I did not feel sorry for him one bit. I still wanted him to pay for what he had done. Then I looked into the camera and shut my eyes and continued to moan in pleasure.

Then I pulled her off of my cock, stood her up and lifted her into the air. I gave her husband a sinister smile as I laid her onto the bed and spread her legs wide open. I then went down on her and stuck my tongue right into her pussy and began eating it out like it was thanksgiving turkey. She immediately began to squeal and moan in pleasure. She slammed her hands onto the bed and began gripping the covers as tight as she possibly could.

My tongue was going full speed all over her pussy. Then I took my finger and slid it into her pussy hole and began finger fucking her while I also simultaneously licked her out. I was going as fast as I could and she was screaming. She began to assist me by air humping while still gripping the sheets.

Then, I stood up, spun around and laid down on top of her in the 69 position. I shoved my cock into her mouth as I picked up where I left off eating out her pussy.

Her screams were now muffled by my cock as it consumed her entire mouth. She continued sucking despite being under the influence of mind numbing pleasure. Her pussy was just oozing and I continued to eat her out nonstop.

Roughly five minutes or so passed and I climbed off of her. Then she leaned up and crawled over to me. I repositioned myself where my dick and legs were facing her husband so he could get a good, clear look at what I was about to do. I looked him in the eye as his wife had now climbed on top of me and said, "Get one last look at your wife, you little bitch because I am about to violate her."

Then, I positioned her on top of my cock in the reverse cowgirl position where she was facing him. I then grabbed my dick and slid it right into her pussy.

His last words were, "No… No… Noooooooo!"

And my response was, "Ohhhh yeah! Yeah! Yeaaaahhhhh!" Just as I began to pound her little pussy out. Her pussy was the best feeling pussy I had ever stuck my dick inside of. It was warm, wet and tight. It was like a perfect massage for my cock.

I was fucking her as fast and as hard as I possibly could – way harder than I had ever fucked before. I wanted him to see his wife receiving the fuck of a lifetime and he saw it – live and in person.

She was moaning so loudly, I knew the whole neighborhood could hear it but I did not care.

I grabbed that tight little ass as I continued to pound her out. She almost couldn't take it. Then, I flipped her onto her hands and knees - with my dick still inside of her – and began fucking her doggie style. We were both facing her husband who sat there like a broken man. Tears were in his eyes as he just stared at us blankly.

Her head was tilted downward so I grabbed her by her pretty hair and snatched her head up so he could see the pleasure that consumed her gorgeous face.

I kept pounding away and noticed her ass cheeks were blood red from my body clashing against them.

I then pulled out and laid her down on her side. I laid down behind her on my side and used my right leg to lift her right leg up. Then I entered her pussy again with my dick and began to pound her in this position. I reached over and grabbed her tits while fucking her in this position. Her pussy felt so great. She was sweating profusely and screaming uncontrollably. I know this was the best fuck she had ever received and far superior to any fucking this bitch of a husband ever gave her.

I kept on fucking her fast and hard. Then I pulled out, grabbed her shoulder and pushed her down onto her back. I was eyeing her tits before I grabbed them, pushing them together and slid my dick in between then and began titty fucking her just as fast and as hard as I was her little pussy that was now beaten out and soaked.

I was drilling those tits fast. She leaned her head up and opened wide, taking in the head of my dick with each thrust. I could have literally done this all night. I loved her tits. Hell, I loved every single aspect of her body. She was simply put: amazing!

I then pulled away and stood up, motioning for her to stand up as well. She did just that. Then, I grabbed both of her legs, spread them wide and lifted her into the air as she wrapped her arms around my neck. I then slid my dick into her and began to fuck her while holding her. Her mouth was wide opened as she moaned and I then took advantage of it by sticking my tongue in her mouth. We made out as I fucked her while holding her.

Her breath tasted so good. It was like a mint with strawberries. Even after sucking on my dick and screaming bloody murder, her breath still tasted fresh.

I began walking around the bed, fucking her while holding her. I then slammed her into the wall and began drilling her against it. I was fucking her so hard, a picture of Marty and her fell from the wall, shattering against the floor. But she didn't even flinch. It was a perfect exclamation mark for what I was doing to both him and her.

I then walked off and stepped down from the bed, still fucking her while holding her. I started circling around him, taunting him even more. The sound of my body clashing against her as I power fucked her while holding her was deafening and it resounded throughout the room along with the haunting screams of his wife in the throes of passion. I then dropped her onto her feet and bent her over the bed right in front of him with her ass facing him. I then stepped behind her and entered her from behind and pounded her out against the bed. I was going nonstop.

All he could see was my bare ass clashing into her. Her face was planted into the bed as she gripped the sheets. Her moans were muffled by the bed.

I was fucking her with all of my might. Sweat was pouring from my body as was her body as well.

I slid my hands down her soaking wet back. I then grabbed her shoulders and lifted her up. Then, while still fucking her from behind, I spun her around facing him as I continued to pound her out as he watched.

I then spun her back around and laid her onto her back. She spread her legs wide as she laid right in front of him. He could clearly see her beaten out, soaking wet and blood red pussy. I then stepped in, slipped my dick back inside of her and began to fuck her while standing there as she laid on her back.

I reached over and grabbed her tits, squeezing them as tight as I could. By now, I was no longer focused on him and completely focused on this gorgeous piece of meat that I was currently devouring. I watched as her eyes were rolled up into the back of her head and her mouth was wide open as she screamed bloody murder, completely consumed by the intense pleasure I was giving her.

I held her tits tight as I continued to fuck her fast and hard. I was preparing for the climax as I could feel it coming.

"You gonna fucking make me cum?" I said. "Huh? You gonna fucking make me cum?" As best as she could, she incoherently uttered, "Uhhhh yaaaaa!"

"Yeah, I'm gonna fucking cum, baby!" I told her.

I fucked her for about another minute or so and then I pulled out. She jumped off of the bed and immediately dropped to her knees. We positioned ourselves perfectly in front of him so that the could see the final shot. I stuck my dick in front of her face and began to jerk it off, building for the final moment.

She opened wide as my dick just exploded, unleashing cum all over her pretty face. I kept cumming and it felt amazing. It was the best orgasm I had ever received by far. I covered her entire face in cum.

And then, it was over.

I looked to her husband and he was catatonic. In a literal state of shock. She crawled before him and just waved her cum soaked face in front of his. I put my clothes back on, grabbed my camera and tripod and exited, patting him on the back on the way out.

On the way home, I stopped and had the recording printed onto a dvd. On the case, I wrote, "Wedding" implying it was my wife and I's wedding dvd that we never had printed. As I got home, I walked in like it was a normal day. She greeted me at the door pretending to be excited to see me and completely unaware that I knew.

I showed her the wedding dvd and her face lit up. She wanted to watch it immediately and I told her to wait. I dumped my stuff off, changed clothes and then instructed her to go ahead and watch it, telling her I had to leave and run some errands. She said she would and would let me know what she thought of it.

And so I left and called Rebecca on the way out. She thanked me for a wonderful time and told me she was in the process of filing for a divorce. Then she asked me if I wanted to see her again tonight to which I agreed.

As soon as we got off the phone, I received a text from my wife saying, "I am so sorry. I don't know what else to say." I simply responded by saying, "There's nothing else to say. I'm glad I caught you because I think I was made for Rebecca and if not for you, I would never have met her."

The Cuckold Watches:
Sharing His Wife Saves His Marriage

After ten years of marriage and hitting the age of 40, my wife and I were officially past the inevitable "settled down" stage: we were practically just roommates who shared the same bed. Due to infertility issues on my part, we did not have the luxury of having kids to sort of respark our lives by adding a new joy to it. We both did not want to adopt simply because we did not want to take on a kid who truly wasn't ours in terms of genetics. So here we were: two roommates who had grown bored with each other. I can't even tell you the last time we had sex because it was ages ago. In fact, I had grown bored with it and she had as well – long before I did of course – and I believe that was the root of our frustrations and problems: the lack of sex. We were both sexually frustrated. She never had a decent sex life with me because sex with me was always boring. It was the same two positions – missionary and her on top – for ten or fifteen minutes and we were done.

I don't know why sex grew boring for me but it was probably due to the fact that I started having serious erectile dysfunctions. I could not get a hard on to save my life so the last few times we had sex, I was only roughly halfway hard and that made horrible sex for my wife even worse.

I knew the inevitable talk would come eventually, I just did not expect it to be so sudden. One day after coming home from work, she greeted me at the door and asked me to sit down. I took a seat beside her on the couch in the living room, knowing where this was going. I just did not know what decision she had made inside of her head.

The odd thing was I saw a glimmer of hope in her eyes – as if she wasn't going to leave me but she found another solution – a more hopeful solution that would result in the both of us staying together. Don't get me wrong, I still loved her and I was certain she may still love me. A divorce was the last thing I wanted. In fact, despite us growing apart, I still couldn't see myself without her.

So she looked me in the eye and that's when the official talk began.

She started by going over everything that has gone wrong in our lives over the past few years. Then she went on to talk about our sex life and the fact that she has certain needs that I simply was not fulfilling and could not fulfill.

That's when she hit me with the last thing I was expecting. She looked me in the eye without hesitation and said, "How would you feel about me exploring?"

"What do you mean about you exploring?" I asked.

"I mean, me having sex with another man." She replied.

At first, I didn't know what to say. Then she practically sat there and convinced me that it was what she needed and she assured me there would be no feelings for said man. She wouldn't leave me for him. She just wanted me to loan her out to him for sex. And so, I thought about it for a second and ultimately figured that it wouldn't hurt anything. As long as it would make her happy, then it would make me happy. So

I agreed to it and that is when she told me she had been browsing the internet for ideas and found a website that takes mature women who were married to men lacking in the bedroom and allows "professionals" to fuck them.

I assured her that I would be fully supportive of whatever decision she makes. That is when she told me that she had already sent a body shot into this company and they approved her before sending her a list of potential candidates. She chose the guy she wanted and they informed her that he was available and willing.

She showed me a picture of him and he was very handsome. He appeared to be tall. He was bald with sharp blue eyes. Judging by a shirtless picture, he was in great shape and had the size of an NFL player. His body was ripped and muscular. I thought to myself that it would be an honor for him to fuck my wife.

They had the date booked for Saturday in an apartment complex downtown. She said that he would allow the husband to tag along and watch if I was up for it and although I had to think about that a moment, I eventually decided that it would be best for me to go and be there to support her. Plus I figured I may learn a thing or two.

And so Saturday rolled around with haste. After staying up all night thinking about it, I drove my wife to the very apartment complex in downtown. Hand in hand, we approached the door and knocked on it.

The very man from the picture opened the door and he was bigger than he looked in the photos. He welcomed us in – including me. He introduced himself as "Eric" right after we stepped in. He stopped and eyed my wife up and down while licking his lips. He looked like a predator ready to feast on his prey.

My wife was starstruck almost. I could tell she was acting shy and coy – just as she used to do around me when we first started dating.

He invited us back to his living room where he asked me to take a seat in a nearby recliner. My wife and Eric took a seat on the couch, side by side. He asked her if she needed anything – such as a drink or snack – but she declined. We knew small talk and conversations that involved getting to know each other weren't allowed and so it didn't take long for him to ask if she was ready and she shook her head with a huge smile.

He then stood her up and began to eye her up and down. Then he slipped her little one piece summer skirt off and she stood there in only her bra and panties. Then he moved in and began kissing her while feeling all over her body.

She closed her eyes and began to breathe heavily as his lips caressed her long and smooth neck. His hands began to massage her breasts before he popped both of her tits out of her bra. He moved down to her tits and began to lick them as if they were a pussy he was licking with momentum.

He began to squeeze them as her body was tensing up. I could tell she was extremely horny. In fact, I hadn't seen her this horny in a long time.

He began sucking on her boobs as one hand slid down to her pussy. He began to gently rub it while continuing to suck her boobs. She began to blow deep, heavy breaths as he continued to toy with her, intensifying her level of horniness.

Then he reached around and began to grab her thick and plump ass, squeezing it as tight as he could. She began to dry hump him, rubbing her lower body across his.

Things were heating up and they were heating up fast.

Then he quickly spun her around, grabbed her panties and yanked them down.

"What a pretty, pretty pussy!" He said before dropping down on his knees, sticking his tongue out and shoving it right into her pussy.

"Ohhhhhhh!" She screamed as she gripped the top of his shiny bald head and jerked her head back in pleasure.

He then stood up, spun her around, bending her over in the process as she had her hands against the couch, propping her up. He bent down again, grabbed her pussy and spread it open before going in and licking it out once again.

She began to squeal as she gripped the couch as tight as she possibly could. Her head was jerking back and forth as she was losing control. Whatever he was doing down there clearly felt amazing and she could only take so much of it. Her head was rocking back and forth as if someone or something else was possessing her.

He then began to lick slow and long licks with his tongue. I could hear her gasping for air as if she was out of breath already. Then he stood up and smacked her on her right ass cheek, leaving a red hand print behind. He pulled his shirt off before then pulled his pants off. The entire time, my wife just stood there, hunched over in the same position as if she was waiting for the grand finale. Then he pulled his boxers off and a monstrous, seven inch cock popped out. It was rock hard and throbbing.

Just as that happened, my wife turned around and her eyes lit up with passion. It was as if she had never seen or imagined one that big before. Of course, she never saw one with me and before me, she hadn't been with many guys so it was obviously the biggest dick she had ever seen. All I could say was she deserved this cock and the fucking that was on its way to her.

"Oh my…" she uttered before dropping to her knees and grabbing it with both hands, jerking it as hard as she could. Then she opened wide and swallowed every inch of his massive cock. She began to suck it in a way she had never sucked mine before. She wanted this cock and she wanted it bad. Her eyes began to water as the head had to have been down in her throat. Then she started to gag but like the champ that she is, she didn't stop. She kept going and kept going. He was moaning with pleasure as he grabbed her hair, gripping it tight.

Then, she finished, gave the head of his huge cock one gentle kiss and stood to her feet. They began to make out again as she stroked his cock in the process. Then, she broke away and he spun her around back in the same position. She bent over and spread her legs wide open, waiting for that massive dick to be shoved inside of her delicate little pussy.

He stood directly behind her and flexed his muscular ass as he grabbed his dick and angled it directly in front of her pussy before slowly sticking it in. Her pussy was so tight combined with his dick being so huge, he had to slowly force it in.

She screamed as loud as she could as he shoved that dick all the way inside of her. Then, without showing any mercy whatsoever, he began to beat that pussy out.

Clap… clap… clap… smack… smack… smack… clap… smack… clap! Is all I could hear combined with the resounding screams she was letting out and the manly growls he was emitting.

This was full on hardcore fucking and as I said, he was showing no mercy. He was hell bent on dominating her tight little pussy with his huge dick and he was doing just that.

He gripped both of her sides tightly as he was pounding her out hard and fast, literally going 90 to nothing as if it was the last piece of ass he would ever have the opportunity to fuck.

She was screaming bloody murder as his massive cock was fucking her like a jackhammer.

He then paused a moment, while still leaving his cock inside of her, took a step onto the couch, bending her down a little further and then began dropping up and down, ramming her with his huge stiff cock.

Her face was now planted into the couch and her screams were muffled. I was watching as his entire body was flexing. It was as if he was working out.

I caught a better look at the action from this position and it looked incredible. Almost primal. Her once tiny little pussy was stretched out to the max by his huge dick. It was soaking wet and blood red. His huge balls were bouncing around everywhere. It was a bizarre yet interesting picture.

He kept dropping down with a boom. Her body was bouncing around from the violent pounds of his body but she was taking it like a champ, not resisting him or his big cock at all.

After a few more minutes passed, he pulled his dick out again, then commanded her to "suck her pussy juice off his dick". She turned around and obeyed him as she swallowed his dick whole again while rubbing her little pussy. She kept sucking for about five minutes before he stood her up and lifted her into the air, spreading her legs wide and dropping her pussy down onto his cock. He then began to power fuck her – hard and fast – while holding her in the air. She was screaming and almost to the point of tears as he ripped her pussy apart. She wrapped her arms around his neck and held on to him as tight as she could as she was undergoing both the ride of her life and the fuck of her life.

He then dropped her down onto the couch and began to fuck her in the missionary position. He ass was flying high into the air as he drove her deeper and deeper into the couch. She was moaning and screaming. Her hands were all over the place. It's as if she literally could not control herself. And then, her eyes rolled into the back of her head as she began to orgasm. When he sensed this, he began to fuck her faster and harder. He was doing it just right, just to intensify her raging orgasm. Her body was tensing up and then she began to tremble until it stopped. He kept fucking her hard and fast. I could see that his dick was soaked.

He then lifted up, picking her up in the process as she began to ride his dick up and down. While she wasn't capable of fucking him as fast and as hard as he was fucking her, she was still bouncing up and down on that dick in a way she had never done before.

Some time had passed and she was now on her back with her legs spread high into the air around his shoulders. He was driving her home – still hard and fast. She was still screaming like she had been doing all day. Another minute passed and she cummed once again. This was twice now where as half the time I couldn't even get her to truly sincerely orgasm just once. It was hell and hard for me to get her to cum while this guy was doing it right away.

He stood up while lifting her up into the air on top of the couch and then planted her back into the wall. Thump! Then he began drilling her while standing. Still, after all this time, he was going 90 to nothing and showing no signs of slowing down.

His amazing body was completely drenched in sweat. All I could see was the back of his muscular and sweaty body along with her head over his shoulder, arms around his back and her legs spread out around both sides of his body.

Her face was wincing in pain and pleasure. She was simply not herself at this particular moment in time. Then, once again, she began to cum. She gripped his body tight as her face dropped and her moaning got lower. Like before, he began to plow her faster and harder, hitting her just right to intensify the orgasm. And it was a success.

This now made three orgasms in one session! I found this to be quite incredible to say the least. He was a champ and he wasn't afraid to show it either!

Some time had passed and he now had her laying on the couch while he stood on the ground, plowing her in this position. He had slowed down with long hard thrusts. I simply sat back and watched as he began talking dirty to her.

And then, he commanded her to get on her knees and she did just that. He pulled his huge dick out which was oozing of her pussy juice as she hopped off the couch and dropped to her knees. He shoved his dick into her mouth and began to fuck her mouth hard and fast.

"Make me cum! Make me fucking cum!" He stated to her.

She began to suck his dick while he simultaneously fucked her mouth. Then he grabbed her head tight, holding it still as his thrusts began to slow. His body tensed up as his muscles upon muscles poked out. His face tightened as his eyes shut and he began to groan as he cummed all inside of her pretty little mouth that I always liked to kiss.

He blew several loads into her mouth before he pulled out. Cum was oozing from her mouth as she fell back into the couch, recuperating from the best and hardest fuck she had ever received. He looked to her and said, "I have a shower if you'd like to clean up. We can even clean up together."

With all her might and catching her breath, she said, "that sounds lovely!"

And so he assisted her up, then threw her over his shoulder as he carried her off to his shower.

It was then I realized that my dick was rock hard. It hadn't been this hard in a long time. I could not believe it! I was happy and ecstatic!

At the end of the day after another fuck session in the shower, we made it back home safe and my wife was still in one piece. She was now happy as was I. He helped cure me of my erectile dysfunctions and from then on out, I had no problems getting a hard on. So it's as if this strange but handsome man Eric cured both me and my wife. He made us both happy again and happy to be with each other!

And with that being said, a new beginning was underway. We both turned the page and started a new chapter… together!

Sharing My Wife With A Porn Star: How I Became A Cuckold

My first time ever being cuckolded… I did not know what to think. How to feel about it. Or what to even do about it. But one thing is for certain: I wanted it. I wanted to sit and watch as my loving wife has her tight little pink pussy stretched out by another man's rod. I wanted it badly. So bad in fact, I could feel it. I could almost taste it…

It all started roughly a week ago when my wife – who was a virgin prior to meeting me, but we'll cover that later on – came to me with the idea. I have always been terrible in bed and I for one am not ashamed to admit that. There are many things I'm skilled at that I am overly proud of and many things to which I am not so lucky at, and sex in the bedroom with a girl is something I was never good at. I loved my wife and had no issues with satisfying her in any way that I could – even if it meant lending her out to another dude. I did not care as long as she was happy and if she's happy then my ass is sure to be happy. She was my princess… on second thought, I was soon to be her and her new man's little princess.

After five years of giving her the worst sex of her life and always having a fantasy of seeing another man fuck her brains out, we finally had the inevitable "talk". The talk that not very many couples in our age range have to face. She sat me down one evening after twenty minutes of a lame sex session and spilled her heart out to me. She said something has to be done because she couldn't take my weak ass sex anymore.

Admittedly, I never told her about my secret fantasies. The fantasies that involved me watching her fuck another man. I did not know how she'd take it. I was afraid she would think I was some freak. Seriously, how would your wife or significant other react to finding out you secretly want to see her fucked by another man? It's borderline insanity… but not for me. It was my fantasy. It was my longing desire.

I wanted it and I wanted it badly. I wanted to see my wife sit down and fuck the hell out of another man right in front of me. I wanted it more than I wanted money. I wanted it more than I wanted success. In fact, it was all I wanted. Hell, I craved it like a starving dog craves food in the garbage dump.

And so, after a long pause as she waited for me to state my case, I finally broke the news to her. I did so in a very timid manner because I did not know how she'd take the news. I did not know how she'd react to it. But looking at her, she didn't roll her eyes. She didn't give me a ball busting look. She didn't pierce me with her eyes.

Instead, she smiled. Her eyes lit up like a Christmas tree. Almost as if this is exactly what she wanted to hear. And then, she dropped the ball on me. She told me her fantasy was to fuck another man. Although it did not involve me watching, she said she would happily and gladly allow me to do so.

Needless to say, it was a relief for the both of us. Little did I know, she had her own secret fantasies as well. So this was just as surprising to me as it was to her.

And so, we had everything arranged. It was going to happen tonight at 8:00pm. Some guy who was an ex porn star she met online was going to be the guest – the guest who was going to fuck my wife right in front of me. To be completely honest, I think I was more excited than my wife was. Hell, I was getting a hard on just thinking about it. In fact, I had to sneak off and jerk my dick three different fucking times throughout the day. That is how excited I was. Just the thought of being able to sit and watch another man's dick enter my wife's little pussy that had only ever been tampered by me was a complete turn on. Hell I was honored – I was honored to have the opportunity and privilege to sit and watch as my wife fucked this man, who happened to be an ex porn star, so it was going to be a show for the ages. A private show that was exclusively for me.

You see, when I met my wife she was a virgin. She was a sexual novice. In fact, she never really truly had a desire to have sex. As I said, I'm terrible in bed so when I first fucked her, she thought it was amazing. But as time went on and nothing changed, she grew wise to my act and realized I was actually terrible in bed, which leads us to where we are today. Both of us were about to get lucky.

So 8:00pm on the dot rolled around. There was a knock at our door. My wife had recently gotten out of the shower and she had "freshened up" every aspect of her body – especially all three major holes – for this man. She was wearing a skimpy little skirt. She answered the door and in stepped Long Rod McAllister. Yep, Long Rod McAllister. That was his porn star name. I didn't bother to research this guy beforehand, but I knew by the name he wasn't going to disappoint.

When he walked through our door, my wife was all smiles. She took him into the living room where he looked at me and smirked. He gave me that look like "how the hell did a loser like you get a hot ass woman like her?" He didn't bother to introduce himself, but instead, told me to sit my ass down. I did and I thanked him for it. I even said, "I'll do anything for you, sir." He just smiled in response before looking my wife in the eyes. Then he grabbed her and tossed her onto the couch, spreading her legs wide open. She didn't have on any panties so it was very easy access for him. He bent down, stuck that long ass tongue out that resembled a snake tongue and started going to town on her little pussy. She started screaming and jerking around, uncontrollably, like she was on a fucking ride at the amusement park.

Honestly, I had never even attempted to eat her out before so this was a first time for her and not even a minute in, she was enjoying every millisecond of it.

Her eyes were darting everywhere as she couldn't keep her body still. She was thrusting his tongue while gripping the couch as her head was going back and forth with great speed.

His tongue was tapping her pussy like a basketball being dribbled. She kept screaming, laughing and moaning. It was a sight to behold and I loved it! This guy was so awesome, I would almost go gay for him. Seriously. He hadn't even started to really fuck her yet and I was already thinking of ways I could repay him. But there was no amount of money worth the experience he was giving both me and my wife here.

He kept licking her out and then began to finger her. His finger was going in and out of her with quick speed as his tongue continued to lick her out as well. Her screaming grew louder and louder. Then suddenly, I got a little worried because something wasn't right. Her eyes rolled into the top of her head as her screams turned into a low moan. Her body began to tremble. It was then I realized he was making her cum. Holy shit! Never in my life was I ever able to make her cum, so needless to say she had never came in her entire life. This was her first fucking time every cumming. It was incredible. I had fucked her for years and never made her cum but this guy made her cum without even putting his dick in her yet.

And so he finally pulled away. He began taking his clothes off and my dick started getting rock hard. My wife laid there, almost out of it. He had worn her out already. Wow!

He removed his shirt and he was in great physical shape. I could literally see every muscle on his body. There wasn't an ounce of fat anywhere to be found on his amazing body. He then removed his pants and underwear and out popped the reason he earned the nickname Long Rod McAllister: it was a dick that had to have been 7 and a half inches. It was long, veiny, throbbing and as hard as it could possibly get. My wife, who could barely move mind you, suddenly shot up in excitement. Her eyes were wide as she stared at his dick agape. Without saying a word, he walked over and just slipped that dick into her mouth. He began to fuck her mouth going back and forth. She truthfully wasn't even sucking it. He was just fucking it and she was taking it – taking it like a true damn champ. Every single inch of that beast, she was taking it with ease.

He kept on pumping that pretty little mouth of hers and the funny thing is, she never sucked my dick. In fact, she never even attempted to because I just honestly wasn't into having my dick sucked. I always preferred the vagina and that was it. Nothing more and or nothing less. I was strictly limited to the pussy and that is all I truly ever wanted. No oral blow jobs, just the pussy.

Finally, after about five minutes of straight drilling her little mouth, he pulled out. His dick was covered in her saliva but he didn't care, neither did she or myself. He grabbed her, stood her up and slipped that skimpy little skirt right off of her. They were both now butt ass naked. Their bodies were both amazing. My wife always had an amazing body. So needless to say, their two bodies were both compatible for one another. They were perfect for each other.

He then spun her around, bending her over onto the couch. Her plump little ass just poked out into the air. He grabbed her legs and spread them out wide. Her pussy sat there wide open and waiting – waiting for him to shove that long ass rod into it. It was moist all over and I could tell it was aching for his humongous dick.

He grabbed that long ass rod of his, angled it directly in front of her pussy and then shoved it in. I could hear that pussy pop as his huge ass dick entered her. She immediately screamed as he rared back and started going to town. He was fucking her at lightening speed. The sounds were just incredible. It was sounds I had never heard before and they were intense. The smacking sounds emitted by his body clashing against her nice plump ass. The moans he was making, The screams she was making. The sound of his dick going in and out of her wet pussy, it was all together combined a masterpiece of music.

With each clash of their two bodies, her plump little ass was just jiggling – jiggling like a water balloon. Her ass was already blood red. But he wasn't close to being finished with her. He continued to dominate her pussy by fucking her as hard as he could at light speed.

He kept going until he pulled out. It was time to swap positions. By not at this point, my dick was rock hard. I was wanting to pull it out and jerk it so bad. I wanted to and it was hard to resist. I didn't want to look like a freak but seriously, I was already a freak at this point considering the situation and the fact that I was willingly allowing it to happen and enjoying it on top of that. But I refrained from whipping it out and jerking off… for now…

And so, he continued by flipping her over onto her side, squatting down and hiking one leg over his shoulder. Then he grabbed his cock and went straight for her pussy, shoving it in. Her little cunt took that cock like it belonged there. And thus, the fucking continued. SMACK! SMACK! SMACK! She started screaming again as she gripped the couch as tight as she could. The couch itself was ramming against the wall with fierce intensity. It was hitting it like a battering ram. BOOM! BOOM!

BOOM! SMACK! SMACK! SMACK!

He started groaning like a wild animal as he fucked her harder and harder, faster and faster. She was bouncing all around like she was on a trampoline almost. This was the ride of her life and I was there to experience it with her like a good husband would. Hell, make that a great husband! How many other husbands would not just allow their wives to fuck other men but also allow them to do it right in front of them? Very, very few, I can assure you of that.

And so he continued slapping the inside of her pussy with his dick like a beast on cocaine. He kept going, fast and hard. It was simply put: amazing.

And then, he finally pulled out. As he pulled out, he groaned deeply. He stood there jerking that long and hard ass cock as he plotted his next move. Then, he sat down on the couch, grabbed her and lifted her up, placing her on top of him. She spread her legs as quickly as she possibly could. Then she squatted down onto his cock and began to bounce up and down, up and down, up and down, up and down. She was riding that thing with pride. She was riding that monster cock like she knew what she was doing. She was enjoying it and loving every second of it — every INCH of that hard ass dick.

She was moaning and screaming like I had never heard her do before as her once tight little pussy took every single inch of his long ass dick. He reached up and grabbed her tits, squeezing them like they were cushions. He was squeezing those tits of hers as she kept jumping up and down on his long ass dick like a mad woman.

He finally stopped her and leaned down a bit, while lifting her plump little booty into the air. Then he began drilling her at light speed. She was still on top only now HE was doing all the fucking once again. His break time was officially over and he was tearing her pussy a new one once again. His dick was fucking the inside of her pussy like a jackhammer. It was going so fast, it was almost a blur. Literally.

He kept on hammering her pussy with his big ass dick. Kept going and kept going until she start cumming once again. I could see her juice falling onto the ground. She was screaming as loud as she could as her body was trembling, not just from the hard fucking he was administering, but from the tremors caused by her orgasm. She finally calmed as he kept going. It's like he didn't give a shit whether she was cumming or not. He was going all in. Non stop and without a single care in the world.

About ten more minutes or so passed and he pushed her off of him. He laid her down onto her back, lifted her legs high into the air while spreading them wide. Then he got in between her with his knees planted into the couch. He quickly slid his dick right back into her pussy and started fucking her again. He was fucking her hard and fast, just as he'd been doing all this time. There was no giving in. No slowing down. No more resting. He was fully charged and still at max capacity. He was fucking her so hard right now, it was literally moving the couch. Slowly but surely, it was moving out of place. If he kept up at this pace and in this position, he would have slid the couch all the way over to the other end of the room. And I'm not kidding you either. That is how hard he was fucking my lovely and beautiful wife.

I just couldn't help but admire this. My wife looked so beautiful, even with that painful expression of intense pleasure on her face. Seeing her with her legs spread wide open with another man's big ass and hard dick going in and out of her like lightening was admirable. Hearing her moan was incredible.

My dick was raging hard at this point. I just couldn't take it anymore. Seeing my wife getting fucked senseless by another man – who happened to be a pro at fucking and also an ex porn star – was just too much to take. I had to do it. I just had to. I no longer cared what they would have thought. Hell, at this point, they had no room to judge me. And so, I unzipped my pants, pulled them down to my knees. Then I pulled my boxers down and there sat my dick. It was so hard, it was throbbing. And to be honest, my dick wasn't a quarter of the size of his big ass rod. It was an ant compared to his but I didn't care. And so, I started jerking it. It felt so amazing. I could only image this is how good it felt for my wife and her lover. Well, probably not that good but close. I kept jerking and it was soooo good.

Their bodies were covered in sweat. Her screams just echoed throughout the room. The couch was moving. His body was clashing against hers. His huge dick was going in and out of her tight – or once tight anyway – little pussy. This was pure art. Art that the world need-ed to see. Art that just couldn't be matched by any other form of art. This was it!

I hadn't even been jerking my dick for a minute and I was already ready to blow. To be honest, they hadn't even noticed me. In fact, I don't think they even knew I was still here. They had forgotten about me a long time ago. I was an after thought. And so the cum was building and then, I blew loads everywhere. It felt so good, I couldn't even keep my eyes open. I kept unleashing cum everywhere and I did not give one single shit. I closed my eyes and kicked back a minute letting my adrenaline wear down. I was almost out of breath. It was an amazing experience for me.

So by the time I opened my eyes, this guy had my wife in a new position already. That was fast. He had her flipped over on the arm rest with her stomach on the arm rest and back in the air as he was on his knees, pounding her out from behind. Still going 90 to nothing and as hard and as powerful as he possibly could.

He was grunting, groaning and making all kinds of crazy noises as she kept screaming and moaning as well.

I pulled my pants back up and buttoned them. Next thing I know, my dick was hard once again. That didn't take long. All these years of struggling to get a hard on and yet, the answer was there all along and I just didn't see it: I had to watch my wife get fucked by another man. It was as simply as that. All this fucking time and this is all it took. Man, oh, man!

He kept plowing her from behind. Fast and hard, Powerful and quick. His ass was so muscular and covered in sweat. And as muscular as it was, it was even jiggling from the hard impact of his body clashing into hers. That's how hard he was fucking my innocent little wife.

He then spread his legs wider and leaned over her with his chest and torso touching her back. His ass was in the air and spread wide open. He had a nice clean asshole, I must admit. Then, with his long ass dick still inside of her, he started hopping up and down like a rabbit. That dick was going in and out of her pussy and I had a bird's eye view of it. Up and down up and down up and down up and down he went! And he was having to go high because his dick was so freaking long. It was like watching a baseball bat in between the legs of some muscular dude just disappear into a woman's pussy – my one and only wife's pussy on top of that.

My dick continued to get harder and harder – especially seeing it from this particular angle. Seeing them go at it like wild animals. Seeing it in such detail and knowing that it was my wife getting plowed by another man. I decided to pull my pants down once again. I was going to jerk off once again. But on this particular occasion, I wanted to make it special. I wanted to cum at the same time as this dude, Mr. Long Rod himself. It was so hard not to touch my dick. It was so hard to refrain from jerking it because I knew if I did, I would blow my load instantly which would ruin my chances of cumming at the same time as this amazing porn star that had his mammoth of a dick going in and out of my wife at the moment.

And so I waited as he continued to drill her to oblivion. My dick was so hard but I had to hold back. Instead, I started to gently rub it. Even then, it made me want to explode. Barely touching my freaking dick! That's the impact these two were having on me.

"Come on, bitch!" He shouted in such a firm tone. Higher and higher he went. That dick was drilling her hard and fast, which was no surprise. I could see those tight, muscular and sweaty ass cheeks tensing up. I could see his entire body flexing. I could tell he was on the verge of going. And guess who else was? Me!

He kept pumping her, hard and fast with great power. My dick was throbbing. I was so ready to explode once again and do so simultaneously with this hunk of a man. He kept going… I kept watching. And finally, he yanked that cock out, spun her around and stuck it in her mouth. She began to suck it as he pumped it. I was on the verge of blowing and I wasn't even jerking off. How pathetic was that?

A few seconds passed and he pulled out of her mouth, grabbed her by the back of her hair, angled the head of his dick right in front of her face and began jerking it. Now was my time. I slowly started jerking my dick while watching him. He kept jerking his long ass dick really fast as I was going slow, trying to pace myself – trying to wait for the perfect moment. I could feel it building up inside of me. It was going fast… and then, he let out a groan and exploded all over her face just as my dick started blowing as well. We were both going at the same time. He was moaning as was I.

Finally, it was over… for all three of us. He quickly dressed himself, thanked her for a great time and then left without even giving me a look. My wife and I both were worn out and exhausted. I laid down beside her on the couch as she put her arm around me with a big smile on her face. I bent down to look at her pussy and it was disgustingly beautiful. It was beaten to hell and back.

My wife then thanked me and asked if she could do it again. I smiled and said, "Only if you allow me to watch." She said without hesitation, "You're always welcomed to watch… and I have someone else willing to come over tomorrow."

Giddily, I couldn't help but smile. I couldn't help but get excited. I wanted this probably more than she did. But it was our key to living happily ever after as a couple. And a new sexual journey for the both of us began…

I'll Be Your Cuckold:
The Real Estate Agent Bangs My Wife

I was approaching 40 years of age and had recently gotten my first adult salary. It took nearly 20 years of full time work, but I finally achieved what I had been working for since I graduated college.

I was married to the woman of my dreams but unlike me, she was a career secretary who barely made over minimum wage – even at the age of 38 herself. Both of our salaries were virtually the same up until I got my big promotion which led to my huge pay raise.

We had spent most of our lives together in a run down apartment complex to which we were eager to escape. Now that we could afford to buy a house, we decided to start house shopping. We finally had the money to do so, so it was time to capitalize.

My wife and I were still madly in love with one another, but our sex life was practically non existent. I started having erectile dysfunctions at the young age of 35 and even with pills (which I'm more embarrassed about admitting I took than admitting I had erectile dysfunctions to begin with), I still could not get a hard on to save my life. We were both satisfied with being each other but when it came to sex, we were both highly unsatisfied. I couldn't help it of course and she knew it. But she was growing lonely in that department and sadly I couldn't satisfy her. We tried everything: her wearing new lingerie around me, watching various porn videos, pill after pill after pill after pill, sex toys, she even studied tricks to do with a man's penis with both her mouth and hands that was guaranteed to get a man's limp dick hard and you guessed it, those tricks didn't work either.

So we were both at a standstill in the department and had basically given up trying. It had gotten so bad, I even told her that if she wanted to be with someone else, even if it was for a night, I wouldn't mind it because she deserved. But she was dead set on not cheating on me. I suppose she would feel guilty about it. But like I said, I wouldn't mind it one bit.

My wife was like fine wine: she got continuously better looking with age. Even at 38, she was still a gorgeous piece of meat – even without make up on. Her body was still tight and smooth. Her ass was just as plump today as it was the day that I met her. Her boobs were the perfect size that every man desires. They weren't too big but they weren't too small. They were just right. They were perfect. Her skin was silky smooth with a slight tan color that every man desired and every woman wanted. Everything about her was all natural as well. She was a beauty. She was a masterpiece. She was the poster child for perfection. She was the every single man on this planet's dream woman. How I ended up with her is anyone's guess. I got lucky to say the least. I was and still am proud of her. I wanted to give her the best life and now that I could afford it, I was going to try my damndest to satisfy her – best I can. Yes, I wish I could satisfy her in the bedroom, but believe me when I say I was going to make it up to her for lacking in that department.

We never bothered to have kids. Hell we never tried for it either. Sure, we will most likely look back on the decision not to have kids and regret it one day in the future but for now, we were happy with that decision. Neither one of us liked kids and neither one of us wanted them which is why we never tried to have any. It was always us and always about us. We didn't want a child to interfere with our lives. I know it sounds crazy and irresponsible, but kids just weren't for us. We were compatible in that department and felt the same about them. We were both responsible people, we just didn't want kids. Simple as that!

And so, after searching for a real estate agent, I came across a guy that the ladies truly loved according to what I read on the internet. His name was Jim Silver the house dealer. Sure, it was a corny name, but he was attractive, built and highly successful in his field. Like I said, the ladies really loved him, plus he was single so I figured it would give my wife a little eye candy to look at in the process.

We met Jim at a home he recommended via email after sending him our preferences and letting him know just exactly what we were looking for. Judging by the pictures, we loved it. It was a modest two story home which was ideal for us as we wanted something a little more spacious with an extra story on top of it. There was a pool and Jacuzzi in the backyard. Not to mention the entire yard – both front and back – was surrounded by a large privacy wall.

My wife of course hadn't seen Jim yet as she didn't bother to look at his pictures as I was in charge of the communications and such so needless to say, she was in for a surprise – a big surprise. He was a sexy man and I was hoping she would enjoy at least looking at him.

As soon as we arrived, he stepped out of his car. My wife was actually in mid conversation and she stopped talking. She went completely mute. I looked over at her and her beautiful blue eyes were locked on him as he stood there waiting for us to step out of the car. Her mouth was open. I could tell already she was in lust with this man. Then she snapped out of her funk and quickly and eagerly stepped out of the car.

I found it odd that he had talked to me the entire time leading up to today, yet he immediately approached my wife first and introduced himself. He struck up a conversation about her and it was as if I was completely invisible to both Jim Silver the House Dealer and my wife. Finally, I had to step in and introduce myself in order to get his attention.

And so he gave us a grand tour of the house and it was perfect. Throughout the entire tour, I could tell he favored my wife as he talked to her more than he did me and there were a few times I caught him blatantly checking her out. In fact, one time, he had his eyes glued on her plump little ass the entire time she was checking out one of the spare bedrooms.

So after the tour, he gave my wife and myself time to talk it over. I couldn't help but notice my wife was acting strange – like she had a secret crush going on and was being very, very coy. I wanted to do my best to make her happy. She clearly deserved it. I finally got her to admit that she loved the house and wanted it badly.

But even while admitting it, it was as if the house was an afterthought on her mind. It's like something else was taking over her thoughts: Mr. Jim Silver the House Dealer. And so, I thought to myself – as crazy as this might sound – it's obvious she finds him attractive and he also finds her very attractive… so I wonder if maybe I could do my wife a huge favor – by having this man please her in both her pussy and the bank account. Surely he was obviously attracted to her, so perhaps, if I offered her up to him, he would give us a discount. I know it sounds crazy, but there was sexual tension brewing between those two and it was obvious. Plus my wife hadn't had sex in a long time, so I was going to do it. Additionally, what's even crazier is I wanted to watch it happen. I knew I'd be turned on by the sheer sight of it.

I made the suggestion to my wife and she downplayed it with a huge smile on her face. But she never rejected the thought. And so, I made her wait there, which was outside before the pool and Jacuzzi. I entered the home to find Jim Silver playing on his phone. Then I straight up asked him what he thought about my idea.

As expected, Jim simply said, "Sure. I'll even throw in a 20% discount." Then he asked if my wife was okay with it and I said "of course she is." I continued by saying, "She's outside waiting for you. And please don't disappoint."

His demeanor suddenly changed to some barbaric alpha male as he said on his way out the door, "Don't you worry about that. She's in for the fucking of a lifetime." He then exited and I trailed behind. He approached her as she stood there smiling shyly. Then, he wrapped his big arms around her and stuck his tongue right in her mouth.

They began making out and I could tell just by making out my wife was hot and horny already. She began feeling all over him as he started feeling all over her as well.

Things were heating up and they were heating up fast. Soon this was about to be so on.

He then broke away and began eyeing her body up and down.

Then he unstrapped her skirt and it fell to the ground revealing her bra and panties.

"I've been admiring your amazing body and it looks even more amazing than I could have imagined." He told her.

Not knowing what to say, she just smiled, batting her horny little eyes. Then he ripped her bra off and began to suck on her titties. She began to moan and breathe heavily as he continued to suck away on her tits like it was the last set of tits on earth. She removed his blazer and button down, revealing he was in great shape. He was ripped and you could see every muscle on his body. Her hands felt all over his muscular chest and his six pack abs. Then she unbuttoned his pants, pulling them down along with his boxers to reveal a massive dick. That monster was damn near seven inches long, rock hard and throbbing. If only mine could ever get that hard and be half as big as his was. It was embarrassing but I was so turned on by it.

Then, he pulled her thong off and began to rub and feel all over her tight little pussy

– that I know was extra tight now considering it hadn't been fucked in ages – and rubbed and felt all over her plump little ass as well.

Then he barbarically lifted her into the air and carried her over to the Jacuzzi, gently placing her down inside of it. She sat against the Jacuzzi wall as he hovered over her with his dick staring her right in the face. Then he dropped down underwater and began to eat her out. She immediately started to freak out as the intense pleasure took over her body instantly. It had been a long time since a man touched her down there so she had a lot built up.

Her arms stretched out and gripped the top of the Jacuzzi as her head jerked back and her mouth opened wide. She began moaning as he kept licking away down there. Then he resurfaced to catch his breath, made out with her a few more seconds and then went down on her again, licking her out. About thirty seconds passed then he resurfaced again, standing face to face with her. I could see it on her face and in her eyes that she was craving his giant cock. Then, he put it in her and began to fuck her wildly. Her head dropped back and her eyes snapped shut. She began to moan in intense pleasure as he was fucking her hard, causing the water to become so wavy, he looked like choppy ocean waves during a storm.

After a few minutes, he then flipped around and allowed her to ride him. She was so desperate and horny for that cock, she was riding him like a champ – in a way she never rode me before. She was doing a perfect job and he was loving every second of it. He moaned and groaned as he reached up, grabbing her soaking wet tits and massaging them. She kept riding as he started sucking on her boobs while squeezing them together.

Shortly after, he picked her up with his dick still inside of her and stepped out of the water and onto the Jacuzzi ledge. Then he jumped into the pool with his dick still inside of her. Both of their heads popped up as he started fucking her in the pool. He was going hard and fast – as hard and as fast as he could. The water was growing choppy and wavy. It was splashing all over the surrounding concrete. This was a fucking for the ages which was basically what he guaranteed.

He swam all around the pool while fucking her, getting one hell of a work out in. My wife was so out of it, I bet she didn't even know what planet she was on. The only thing she knew to do at this moment was moan incoherently.

He then swam over to the steps – with his dick still inside of her mind you and humping her in the process – and stepped out of the pool, power fucking her while walking up the steps and back into the house. Water was everywhere from the splashing and plus there was a trail of water leading to the house.

Inside of the house, he took her into the kitchen and dropped her ass onto the counter which was a perfect angle for him. With her on the counter and him standing there, he kept his dick in her and began to drive her home while standing there. He was still fucking her fast and hard. No time to slow, stop or rest. He was a fucking machine. Literally.

His knees were clashing into the counter, causing a loud knocking sound. Combine that with the sound of his dick going in and out of her pussy, the sound of her slapping her hands all over the counter and his body uncontrollably also with the sounds of his moans, groans and grunts along with the sounds of her moans and squeals, this was a fucking pornographic orchestra.

Their bodies were soaking wet and water was all over the kitchen floor and cabinets. But neither one of them cared. I couldn't help but think that in the future, if I were to spill water on the ground in that very kitchen, she would be irate.

However, with him intensely fucking her and getting water from the pool all over the kitchen, she doesn't even give a shit. Hell, she doesn't even care or notice.

He kept on drilling her as she moaned crazily and insanely. Then, he lifted her off of the counter and began to power fuck her while holding her. Her body was crashing into his and it was loud. She was loving every second of it and he was as well.

A few more minutes passed and then he walked over to the stove and dropped her down onto it. It was off of course and thankfully but to be completely honest, all four eyes could have been on and blazing hot and she wouldn't have noticed. That is how out of her mind she was due to his intense fucking.

He then climbed on top of the stove and spread her legs wide. He dropped his dick inside of her pussy and began to fuck her on top of the stove – the very stove that we will one day cook on. How fucking crazy is that?

They were going back to the primitive with this wild and crazy fuck session. It was like watching a live wild porno right before my very eyes and I was enjoying it almost as much as they were – okay, perhaps not quite as much, but I was really into it.

The entire stove was shaking like an earthquake. He was dropping bombs down into her that was ratting the stove. Even the nearby cabinets were rattling from his impact.

Shortly after, he got up, slid her off of the stove and back onto his dick, then he carried her away while power fucking her in the air and walking at the same time. As I said before, this man was a machine. I ran over to the stove just to check and make sure that it wasn't turned on by mistake. Thankfully, it wasn't.

And so I pursued them, following them back into the living room where he was standing in the middle of the room – just in front of the couch – fucking her in the air. He was just standing there, powerfully lifting her up and clashing her into his body. At this point, I couldn't tell if they were still wet or if they were covered in sweat. They were going at it so crazily, it was truthfully hard to tell. I certainly couldn't!

He power fucked her for roughly six more minutes and then dropped her down onto the couch. He climbed on top of her and spread her legs wide in the air and began to drill her, hard and fast. Still, even at this point, this machine of a man was showing no signs of slowing down or growing tired. He was a phenomenal specimen to say the least. The Jacuzzi alone would have worn me out. There is absolutely no way I could have done 20% of all the things he had done up until this point.

I took a seat over on the nearby recliner, kicked back and watched in enjoyment. The recliner itself was actually pretty comfortable – more so than the one we already had. I watched and had a perfect view of the fuck session taking place on my couch. Even envisioned this becoming a thing – ya know, seeing my wife get fucked by other men as a hobby. I had the perfect spot to view it all from.

Meanwhile, Mr. Silver the amazing wife fucking house dealer was still going to town on my wife. His body started tensing up and I could tell he was close to blowing his load. Then he pulled out, crawled up and hovered his cock above my wife's face.

Then he dropped it into her mouth and began humping it while saying, "Suck that pussy off my cock. Yes! Make me fucking cum! Make that fucking dick cum! Right fucking now! Make it cum! MAKE IT MOTHER FUCKING CUM! Work for that discount you whore! Work for it by making me cum…"

A smile flickered across my face. I was absolutely loving this.

He kept humping. His ass cheeks were flexing. They were covered in water… or sweat. Then he began to growl. He closes his eyes and began grinding his teeth.

"Oh yeah!" He began to shout repeatedly. "That is right, you dirty little whore. You just made my dick cum! You just worked for that fucking discount, didn't you? Fuck yes! Ohhhhhhh yes!"

Then he snatched his dick out and began to masturbate, cumming all over my wife's pretty face. It was like he was a cum dumping machine that would not stop. He literally and completely covered her entire gorgeous face in his very own sperm. Her face was glowing off white from all his cum. It looked like someone took a bomb of whip cream and threw it at her face.

Then he finally slowed to a stop. He stood up, with his dick still rock hard, looked at me and said, "Let's get the paperwork signed."

Like it was nothing, he carried on. I looked to my wife who was laying there borderline catatonic and gave her a smile.

A few minutes later, Jim Silver the House Dealer returned with the paperwork and fully dressed like it was nothing. As if he never destroyed my wife's innocent little pussy. I then signed everything I needed to sign – as did he.

With a 20% discount, my wife and I officially became the proud owners of a brand new home all thanks to Jim Silver the House Dealer, his lust for my wife and his big ass monster cock!

Making Him A Cuckold:
How I Banged a MILF In Front of Her Husband

After hitting my quarter life crisis a tad bit later than the average single male, I realized I was at a standstill in life. It was time for a reevaluation. It was time for a change. It was time for a new spark. I needed to find something and I needed to find it fast.

Here I was, sitting at 30 years old, working a dead end job, struggling to make ends meet and on top of that, I was single. It was so hard at this age to find the right chick. The perfect ones were already taken while the rest came with baggage – and plenty of baggage at that. They were either already married, already had kids, lazy, whatever negative aspect about them you could name, they had it.

Most of my friends had married off and the ones who weren't married were either engaged or in love. They were all pussy whipped and had zero time for me. It was a sad time to be alive. I had recently reflected on all the good times I had in my life.

Good times spent with friends, good times spent with girl-friends, the road trips, the parties, everything exciting was all gone. Now it was simply me and practically an empty one bedroom apartment I came home to every night. That was it. Nothing more. Nothing less.

Not knowing what to do with my life or where to go from here, I knew I had to find something. And so, I decided to peruse a few internet ads, just to see what I could come across. Just to see if there was anything interesting. And believe me when I say I wasn't disappointed.

I came across a very shady and vague ad that caught my attention. The title caught my eye right off the bat. It read, "Middle aged husband seeking a man for my middle aged wife. $ $ $ $ $ $ $!"

At first glance, I didn't exactly know what to think about this or truly what it meant and so I decided to click on it to see the details behind it. And this is what the ad read:

"Good evening! To whomever reads this, I am assuming you're

a male and you are looking for sex. If so, then you've come to the right place. I am a middle aged man who is looking to spice up a relationship that has hit a brick wall with my wife of 20 years. Even though she is 50, she is still just as hot today as she was when I met her in her late 20s. My wife and I are both unsatisfied with one another but there is nothing more that I can do to please her. In order to save our relationship, I began reading relationship saving techniques online and the one that keeps hitting home is "cuckoldry can help better a relationship." And so, we have decided to give this a try. We have both agreed to it and feel this is the perfect way to spice up our relationship. I am turned on by the idea of seeing my wife have sex with another man and she is turned on by it as well. So if you would like to get paid to have sex with my wife and don't mind doing it right in front of me, then this is a job that is perfect for you. Please respond to this ad and include a shirtless picture of yourself and of course a little bio along with your age, height and weight. If we feel you are right for this gig, then we'll get in touch with you. Your pay will be determined by your performance and believe me, we won't short you! Hope you'll consider giving this a try! Good luck and hope to hear from you soon!"

I'll admit, it took a second for this to register. When it finally did register, I sat back and thought heavily about this. I thought about "could I actually do this? Am I desperate enough to do this? Will I sink that low? Can I actually perform in front of another man?" My body was decent but nothing special. I hadn't worked out in forever but I was still somewhat fit. My dick was above average and believe me, I wasn't ashamed of it. But could I do THIS? I needed the money and I knew I could please her because that was one thing I was good at: fucking women to perfection. But would I be able to handle doing a married woman and doing it in front of her husband on top of that? And so I spent the rest of the night and all day the next day thinking about it. I even got some advice from some guys I work with and of course, they were all for me doing it. And we did keep it on the down low.

And so after I got off work, I decided I would submit just for the hell of it. By now, I figured they had found their guy but I was going to do it anyway, just to see if I could get a response. I figured everything would be morally okay since they feel they were doing it for a good cause: to better their own relationship. So to help clear my conscious, I just kept telling that to myself.

After getting home, I decided to do some pushups and sit ups to make my muscles look a little more pumped. I did that and then took a shirtless photo of myself and uploaded it onto my laptop. Then, I submitted the picture.

By now, I honestly thought I wouldn't hear back. I figured it was too late. I figured other desperate and horny guys who were into that crazy shit would have pounced on it. But literally, not even five minutes after I submitted the photo, I got a response…

"We like what we see – and my wife does as well. Are you available Saturday at 5:00pm?"

My jaw hit the floor. I didn't know what to say, how to react, how to respond! A thousand thoughts were rapidly flooding my mind. This was it! I was really going to do it!

And so I responded, "Yes! I am available!" Then he forwarded me the details such as his address and phone number along with a very provocative photo of the wife and she was smoking hot! He also noted just above the photo "There's a lot more to come…"

And so I was officially locked in. I was really going to do it. I was going to fuck some stranger's wife right in front of him. Was this weird? Hell yes! Did I care any more? Hell no! She was smoking hot, neither one of them minded – in fact, this is what they wanted – and I felt as if I was doing a good deed to spice up their dull marriage. So I couldn't wait!

And so after days of anticipation leading up to it, Saturday finally arrived and I was showered and freshened up an headed over to this wonderful couple's house. When I arrived in their neighborhood, I couldn't help but notice how big these houses were. They had to be from the six figure range all the way into the million dollar plus range.

That's how big they were. And so they were obviously rich and obviously I could potentially earn a lot of money if I did this right and not screw it up. So I couldn't help but wonder what this couple did? Why they were rich? Who was the rich one? Was it the husband or was it the wife or was it both? I know that didn't matter but I couldn't help but think about it. I also wondered is this what all rich people do? Do they all partake in kinky shit like this? Who knows? All I knew was this couple did and I was going to be the guy who fucks a man's wife right in front of him.

As I pulled into their driveway, I was in awe to see a three story house. It was beautiful, large and fairly new. I got out and walked up to the door and rang the doorbell. Not even a second later, a butt ass naked man with a micro penis answered the door. Yes, this was awkward but it was obviously part of the job and of course, they were already ready – or at least he was. He introduced himself and invited me in like it was nothing. I could tell by the high pitch in his voice that he was excited.

He was jumping around like he was anticipating seeing this more than I was anticipating actually fucking her. How weird is this shit?

And so he escorted me to the living room where his wife was laying completely naked on the couch holding a wine glass. He introduced us as she stood up and shook my hand. Then, he set back and said, "Whenever you're ready, you can begin!" With a massive, ear to ear smile on his face. I could see his little dick starting to rise as he sat there staring a hole through us.

I said to myself, "Here we go! Make this one count!"

His wife was super hot. A perfect ten. I mean she had the most perfect perky tits, a slim stomach, a tight but plump ass and smooth legs that could melt any man's heart. She was hotter in person than she was in the picture and let me tell you, she was the type that obviously gets better looking with age. She was a literal dime piece!

And so I immediately snatched my shirt off and then wrapped my arms around her. She just gazed into my eye's and I immediately dove in for a kiss. I shoved my tongue into her mouth and began to

French kiss her as I started feeling all over her boobs.

She began to unbuckle my belt and unbutton my pants.

I then advanced my hands down onto her ass and began to grab and slap it. By now, she was pulling my pants and boxers down and my big ass dick was standing straight up. She began to grab and jerk it. Then I went straight for her pussy with my finger and began to finger her as I stood there making out with her. Her pussy was hot and wet already. She was already moaning with pleasure as I finger fucked her tight little hairless pussy. Her hands were jerking my cock like a goddess. It felt amazing.

Then, I picked her up, walked over to the couch and dropped her down beside her husband so he could get a close up view of what I was about to do to his wife. I spread her legs high in the air and dove down, shoving my tongue into her pussy. I began to eat that thing out like it was the last pussy I'll ever eat. She began to moan and breathe heavily as she reached over and grabbed her husband's arm for support. Then I shoved my finger into her pussy and began to finger fuck her as I simultaneously at her pussy out with my tongue. It was multi tasking at its finest!

She was moaning, groaning and breathing up a storm and I kept going. I was getting more fierce and intense with it. She almost couldn't take it anymore. Then I stood up, grabbed her by the head and forced her face into my dick. She opened wide and began to suck my dick like a queen. She was massaging it with both her hands and lips. My body began to quiver as it felt so good. I couldn't even keep my damn eyes open! She kept sucking away as now I was the one who was moaning, groaning and breathing up a storm in pleasure.

Finally, she broke away, laid on her back and spread her legs wide. I knew it was time — it was time to do the nasty and get it on with this smoking hot fucking wife! And I did just that!

I squatted down, grabbed my big dick and inched it closer to her wide open pussy. The husband bent over to get a closer look. I could tell he was clearly enjoying this which was a plus for me.

I then slid my dick into her pussy and began to light it up with intense speed and fury. The couch was rocking against the wall and she was now screaming at the top of her lungs. Her body was bouncing into the couch due to the hard fucking I was giving her as the couch continued to clash against the wall.

The husband bent in even closer getting a look in great detail. Then he began to masturbate his tiny little penis as his eyes widened in enjoyment.

Me on the other hand? I just kept fucking away! This was pure ecstasy on my cock! I had never been with an older woman before but this was phenomenal. Her pussy felt better than a fucking 19 year old virgin pussy did.

Her husband kept jerking off as I kept pounding his wife's little pussy as she moaned with her eyes sealed shut. I reached down and began to grab her titties as tight as I could without completely busting them. I was feeling all over them and squeezing them as tight as I could. Then I just couldn't take it anymore and so I pulled my dick out, crawled onto the couch and squatted down on top of her stomach. Then I grabbed her tits and squeezed them together and slid my dick into her tits and began to titty fuck her. I started titty fucking her just as hard and as fast as I was doing her pussy and she fucking loved it. I looked over at her husband who had his mouth hanging down wide open and he was borderline drooling. So obviously he was loving and enjoying it as well, thankfully because I also had to please him as well if I wanted a decent paycheck after I finished up pleasing his wife.

I kept pounding away on those titties and she bent her head down and opened her mouth wide, catching the head of my dick with her lips with each thrust. I looked over to see her husband was still staring wide eyed in amazement. I obviously had won him over already as well. Now I had to continue working on the wife.

And so I finally pulled away from her tits and then I turned her around on her stomach. With her ass hanging over the edge of the couch, I stood above her and dropped my cock down into her pussy and began pounding her like a jackhammer, dropping up and down on her pussy.

I looked up over at the husband to see he had his eyes squinted. Then he suddenly began to nut everywhere and was moaning in the process. For some reason, it turned me on and motivated to fuck his wife even harder and wilder – and so I did. I began to fuck her as hard as I had it in me and as fast as I could. I was dropping my cock up and down up and down up and down up and down. Then, as I continued to fuck her, I began to play around with her asshole with my fingers. I could hear her start to squeal with her moans. She obviously liked it. And then, all of a sudden, I felt her pussy clinch my dick tighter and before I knew it, she was cumming herself. And so that motivated to keep on fucking her with might and power. With my dick still inside of her, I bent down and spread her legs even wider. I commanded her to reach back and grab my neck. She did just that and I lifted her up into the air, with her back connected to my stomach and chest and with her in the air, I began to pump her up and down on my dick. I walked over to her husband and stood before him – like literally right in front of him – so he could get a great, up close and personal view of me fucking his wife.

Both of our bodies were sweaty already and she was sliding all over me as I pumped her up and down on my dick right in front of her husband.

I then backed off and placed her onto the ground, face first. I bent down and grabbed both of her legs and lifted them into the air. I spread them wide open and slid my dick into her pussy and began to fuck her, from behind with her legs spread high and wide into the air. I was standing there while her face was planted into the carpet on the ground as I continued to tear her pussy out from behind. I was fucking her hard and just kept going.

Her husband crawled off of the couch and walked over getting very close to the action. He began to feel his wife's plump and nice ass as I continued to fuck her pussy with all my might. He started doing as I did earlier and began to finger and play around with his wife's asshole as I kept drilling her pussy from behind. And shortly after, her pussy clinched my dick tightly and she began to cum once again.

After she finished cumming, I escorted her back over to the couch and into the position I had her in previously on the couch. Then I spread her asshole wide open and shoved my dick into her tight little asshole and began to pound it out. BOOM!

BOOM! BOOM! BOOM! I was dropping those dick torpedoes right into her tight little asshole. I looked over at her husband and once again he was jerking off just as he was doing before. I kept fucking his wife in the ass and judging by the way he was staring, I don't believe she had ever been fucked in the ass before. But believe it or not, surprisingly she was taking it quite well. Like a champ as a matter of fact. As I was fucking her in the ass, I decided to bend down and finger her pussy in the process. And oh let me tell you, she liked this shit. I kept finger fucking her fast with three fingers as my dick pounded out her asshole. And then, I could feel her pussy clinch my fingers as she began to cum once again. This made three fucking times. I looked over and low and behold her husband was cumming once again as well. So they basically both came simultaneously which was probably another sick desire and fantasy they both wanted.

As I finished up with her ass, I lifted her off of the couch and laid down on my back, allowing her to get on top of me. I wanted to see what she was made of now. I wanted her to ride me and I wanted to see how well she could do it. And so she did just that. She spread those legs wide open, opening up that beautiful little pussy as it bloomed like a rose, then she dropped down onto my dick, swallowing it whole with her pussy and began to bounce up and down like a crazy woman. She was grabbing my shoulders and flinging her hair all over the place.

The husband stood up and got down on his knees on the ground right beside us. He moved in closer to see my dick stretching out his wife's pussy lips as she continued to bounce up and down on it. She kept going and I simply just laid there and relaxed, allowing her to take control and let me just tell you: it felt fucking great. She rode my dick like a fucking professional cowgirl in a rodeo. She was that fucking good – hell I'd even say she was better! Seriously!

I reached up and began to hold on for dear life by grabbing her tits and squeezing them as hard as I could without hurting them. They were my "oh shit handles" to grab on to. I held on to them tight as she kept riding away like a champ!

I continued to let her ride my dick for a few more minutes and then I threw her off of me and onto her back. Then I grabbed my hard dick and stood above her mouth. I looked her in the eye and said, "I want you to make me cum right fucking now!"

She opened her mouth wide and I dropped my dick into her mouth and began to fuck it. I kept on fucking it and fucking it and fucking it. She then reached up and began to play with my balls. It tickled to the point where it was making me want to cum. I could feel it brewing. And then, I pulled my dick out and dumped a load of cum all over her face. When I was done pumping all the cum out, she then opened her mouth and started to suck my dick clean, getting all the remaining cum out and making sure I leave with a clean dick. When it was all said and done, I pulled out and just had a look at both of them. They both sat there in amazement, loving everything I just did! I must admit, I was loving it as well. At first, I wasn't sure about this cuckold thing but if you ask me, I enjoyed it and may have found a new niche.

I wasn't sure what to say but I began to put my clothes back on as I waited on them to make the first move. Then the husband stood up and walked off. The wife just laid there, trying to catch her breath and letting everything that just happened to her process.

A few minutes later, I was fully dressed as the wife was still laying there recovering. By now, she had managed to wipe most of the cum from her face. Then her husband rounded the corner and presented me with a check.

"Thank you!" he said to me. "Seriously, I can't thank you enough. This was an amazing experience for both me and my wife. In fact, I have a proposition I'd like to discuss with you."

"Let's talk!" I said in response to him.

Then he continued on by saying, "I was overly impressed with your performance today and needless to say, my wife was as well, so I was wondering, how would you like to make this a weekly occurrence? You come over and allow me to watch as you fuck her and I pay you exactly what you made today – plus incentives and other goodies."

Of course, I had to take a second to think about this. I had such a great experience as well but I wanted to make sure it was worth it. And then, I looked at the check he presented me with to see that it was written out for five freaking thousand dollars. Are you kidding me? Just for this? A weekly arrangement for five thousand dollars? Hell yes I was down for it!

"Absolutely, sir!" I said to him. He just smiled in response and said, "How does the same time and day next week sound?"

And I answered with a big grin on my face, "It is a deal, sir! I shall see you guys then!"

The Unsuspecting Cuckold:
My Wife Fucks Her Boss and Gets Gangbanged

Our anniversary was approaching and it was approaching fast. It was meant to be a special anniversary because it marked ten years of being married to one another.

Recently, my wife and I had been slowly drifting apart. Although we never mentioned it to one another, we both knew. We could see it in each other's eyes every time we were around one another. It was sort of an awkward tension that neither one of us wanted to address. We never fought and I honestly have no clue what ultimately led to us drifting apart, but I think it had more to do with the fact that we were unable to spend time with one another. It was something that was against our will that neither one of us could control.

Here lately, she had been working like crazy going in at eight in the morning and working until after nine at night – and she was doing this seven days a week. So when she came home late at night, I was either in bed and if I wasn't, she immediately showered and went straight to bed. So needless to say we barely had any time to talk.

I was hoping this upcoming anniversary would be special enough to bring us back together. To ease the tension and alleviate some of the stress that had been brewing between us.

Tonight was the big night. We were supposed to dine in at our favorite restaurant – which was the place we both went on our first official date together. It was a fancy, upscale couple's restaurant in downtown on the rooftop of a luxurious hotel that overlooked the city (the restaurant itself was open to the public and not limited to just the hotel guests). It was a very romantic spot and the fact that it was atop a roof overlooking the dazzling city lights made it even more breathtaking. We hadn't been here in years and I made the suggestion hoping it would be the spot to kickstart our marriage back into high gear – a gear we hadn't seen in a very long time.

I got off work at five and beat her home - which wasn't too much of a surprise. She was supposed to be off at five as well but I simply figured she was forced to stay behind or got caught up in the nightmarish traffic around here.

I went ahead and showered and got ready, sporting the best suit and tie I had. I simply could not wait! 6:30 rolled around and I noticed she still hadn't made it home yet. I was beginning to grow worried now because she should have been home by now. I feared the worst but hoped for the best.

I decided to text her to see where she was because there was no way we'd make it there by 8 – which was the time our reservations were set for. I waited around a minute and didn't get a reply back. Now I was overly concerned and was preparing to go out searching for her. Just before I could leave the house, I received a text back saying she was very sorry, but couldn't get off of work in time. She said she had been meaning to text me to let me know but had been so busy, she couldn't stop to do so.

I admit, I was a little disappointed but I wasn't going to allow her job to ruin our anniversary and further tank our once oh so happy marriage. So I decided I would stop and buy her a dozen roses and hot and freshly glazed donuts (because roses and hot glazed donuts were her favorite things in the world). I did just that and made it to her office around 8:00pm, which was the time we were supposed to be eating at our favorite restaurant. Yes, it was sad she couldn't take off for our anniversary but I was going to make her forget all about it.

Before heading up to her office, I called and cancelled our reservations. Then I took the elevator up to her floor.

As soon as the shimmery elevator doors slid open, I could hear the soft sound of a low moan resounding throughout the office. I couldn't figure out what it was or where it was coming from. The lights in the office were dim and it was quiet other than the consistent moaning.

I followed the moan and the closer I drew to my wife's private office, I realized that's where the sound was coming from. I made it to the door to see that it was cracked open. I took a deep breath and had to force myself to peek inside. Inside my head, I knew what was going on but I didn't what to believe it. I was in a brief state of denial but not for long.

I looked inside of her office and low and behold, to my surprise, there was my wife on all fours on top of her desk getting plowed from behind by some guy. I couldn't tell who the hell he was yet because all I could see was a bare back and a nice, manly ass – far more nicer than my flabby, out of shape ass.

He was hitting her hard and fast – which I could tell she was fighting not to moan as loud as she could or louder than she actually was.

He kept on fucking her from behind while she gripped the desk as tight as she could. This was horrific to watch but I simply couldn't turn away.

And then, the man spoke by saying in a commanding and dominant tone, "You want a fucking promotion? Show me how much you want that fucking promotion!"

And then she just squealed, "Yeaaaaahhhhhh" as loud as she could.

That's when I realized the man who was fucking her from behind was her boss – another man who was married and had two kids. This sort of angered me at first because she had done so much for him and I had invited this man and his wife and kids over to our house on several occasions for get togethers and such. And yet, this is how he repays me by fucking my very own wife. At this point, if I was attractive, confident and in shape, I would have left, marched right on over to his house, dismissed his kids and then fucked the living hell out of his very own wife just go get back at him. But that scenario was clearly out of the equation because I was out of shape, insecure and unattractive. I could see why my wife would want him over me.

By this point, he had flipped her around on his back, climbed up onto the desk in a squatting position with his dick still inside of her and he was bouncing up and down. I could see her pussy a little better now- despite it consuming a huge dick – and it was soaked and blood red from being beaten out by his dick which looked to be seven inches long.

I'm not quite sure how long they had been fucking, but I could tell it had been a while.

Both of their bodies were covered in sweat and they were both breathing heavily.

At first, like I said, I was a little shocked and angered, but the more I watched, the more I realized I was slowly turned on by it and couldn't look away. I even noticed I was getting a hard on – and here of late, that is another issue I was having – erectile dysfunctions. But that's for another time and place.

He stood back on the floor as he was preparing to cum. My wife climbed down on the ground as he jacked off in front of her face, exploding his sperm all over wide open mouth.

I couldn't ever recall my wife allowing me to cum in her mouth as she was strictly against it and was grossed out by it. But not anymore.

I realized since they were finished that I needed to get out of there as quickly as I could and I did just that.

Back at home, my wife hadn't returned yet. I quickly ditched the roses and ate the donuts before heading to bed. I didn't want her to know that I knew. Of course, I didn't know what to do. My wife was no longer innocent and had proven herself to be unfaithful. A lot of unanswered questions were answered tonight. I decided I was going to keep my mouth shut on the issue and just see how things turn out from this point forward.

Eventually, my wife came home. I laid there, pretending to be asleep as she tip toed through our room and into the bathroom. She took a shower and prepared herself for bed before silently slipping into bed. The entire time, I still pretended to be asleep.

She flipped the light off without saying a word to me and closed her eyes. I didn't know whether to feel betrayed or not. It was our anniversary and she couldn't even wake me up to say that she loved me. And so we both went to sleep. This was definitely one hell of a way to end our five year anniversary.

The next morning I woke up to discover my wife wasn't in bed. I got out of bed to discover her car was gone. I checked my text messages to see where she had sent me a message saying she had to work again. She apologized for not telling me this but also said she did not want to wake me up so early in the morning.

After what I uncovered the night before, I knew what she was doing but of course, I did not want her to know that I knew so I refrained from calling her out. I simply told her to have a good day to which I received no response back.

So I quickly got ready to head back over to her office. Inside, what I saw the night before really turned me on and I wanted to see more. I loved seeing my wife pleased and if I couldn't do it, then I loved seeing another man do it.

I rushed over to her office and hopped on the elevator. I could only imagine what I was going to see. As those familiar shimmery elevator doors slid open, I noticed the office lights weren't dim today. I also noticed that there were no low sounds of moaning coming from my wife while in the throes of passion.

I stepped up to her office door and it was unusually quiet. I thought for a second that perhaps they were taking a break or were in between fuck sessions. I peeked through her door to discover she was actually at her desk working. This was unusual and maybe just as shocking as seeing her fucking another man the night before. No one else was around and she was glued to her desktop computer, expertly typing away.

I did not want her to see me so I quickly and silently left.

I sat in the parking lot in my car for a while, trying to make sense of this situation. Was I imagining last night? Was I in some way dreaming? None of it made sense. I continued to sit there dwelling on the bizarre situation. It was then I saw my wife leaving and approaching her car. I hid behind the steering wheel, but peeked over just enough to watch her. By now, it was around lunch time and she told me she would be working all day. So I figured she was simply going to grab a bite to eat. She was alone and no one else was with her or following her out. Despite that, I decided to tail her anyway. I kept my distance so she wouldn't see me or become suspicious because the last thing I wanted her to know was that I knew what she was doing.

I ended up following her into a middle class subdivision just on the outskirts of the city. I parked a few houses down where she wouldn't notice me but also close enough to where I could see her. Obviously, she wasn't going to grab a bite to eat unless someone she knew was cooking for her at home. This wasn't her boss' house as he and his family had a much nicer house. In fact, I had no clue as to who the hell lived here.

I watched her get out of her car and approach the door. She rung the door bell and stood there a moment before the door opened. I noticed it was one of her male coworkers by the name of Dan. They both smiled at each other and said a few words before she stepped inside. I could not tell what they said to one another.

I didn't know Dan very well. I heard her only mention him a few times and I only spoke with him briefly at different company parties her and I attended together.

I decided to step out of my car and sneak over to their house. I stepped onto his property and basically tip toed across his lawn. I peeked through the living room window to see if I could see anything but did not see them nor did I notice anything unusual or out of the ordinary.

I made my way over to the side of his house and peeked through one of the windows. It as the window to a bedroom and neither one of them were in there either. Just as I started to step away, I noticed the door flung open and low and behold, my wife and Dan were tangled up in each other's arms, making out as they made their way into the bedroom.

My wife's dress shirt was already off of her and she was wearing her glue on bra. She still had her skirt on but not for too much longer. Dan was already shirtless as well.

There my wife was – a once innocent girl now turned into dirty little slut in no time. This was the second man (that I at least knew of) that she had been with in less than 24 hours. Color me surprised!

He slammed her into the wall as she stood there with her arms raised. I saw him give a desperately horny look at her as if he was a predator about to devour his prey. She was breathing heavily and I could tell she was just as horny as he was.

He began to lick her neck and licked her all the way down to her belly button. Then he slid her skirt right off of her to reveal she wasn't wearing any panties. I could see that bare, hairless pussy was just aching for Dan's horny cock.

He bent down even further and began to lick her little pussy clean. Her eyes rolled into the back of her head as she opened her mouth and began moaning.

He licked her for about a minute before rising and taking off her bra. Then he firmly grabbed both of her perfect little perky tittles and began to massage them before taking them both in his mouth. I could tell she was clearly enjoying this as well.

Then she broke away and unbuttoned his pants, taking them off along with his underwear to reveal a nice, hard and throbbing cock just ready to fucking the living shit out of her.

She bent down and grabbed his cock and began to jerk it. I saw her look up and smile at him before she opened her mouth wide and swallowed every inch of it. His head leaned back as he began to groan. I could hear him saying, "Oh yeah," in such a sinister and stimulating tone.

My wife could give great head, I admit, but she never once gave me head that felt as good as it obviously did to Dan. Apparently she had been holding out on me.

She sucked his dick for about ten minutes before they moved onto the bed. She climbed on top and spun around as they began to 69 one another. I could see him eating out her pussy like a pro while she sucked away giving him just as much pleasure as he was giving her. They remained in this position for about ten minutes before she spun back around and faced him while on top of him still.

She spread her legs wide as his dick was standing straight up and throbbing. He grabbed it as she lowered herself down, hovering her wide open pussy lips just above it. And then, she sat down on it taking it all in. She moaned loudly just as his rock hard dick entered her tight little pussy. She began to jump up and down up and down up and down as if she was on a trampoline. She was moaning fiercely as he groaned and grunted in sheer pleasure while fucking his dick.

He was grabbing on to her tight as she had her hands planted on his manly chest. Then, as she continued to ride his dick, he reached up and began firmly massaging both of her tits once again. As she kept riding his dick, he grabbed her and pulled her upper body down and opened his mouth wide and began to suck on both of her tits as she continued to ride him.

After a moment, he leaned up which forced her to lean up as well. They were both sitting upright as she continued to fuck his dick. Meanwhile, he was sucking away on both of her perfect little titties.

Then he stuck his tongue out and looked up at her with menacing eyes. It's as if she could read his mind because she opened her mouth wide and he leaned over and shoved his tongue right into her mouth. They began making out while she continued to ride his dick like she was on bike.

She eventually pulled away and slid down on him. He just laid there with his hard and soaking wet dick from her pussy juice staring right at the ceiling. She moved down to his dick and began to suck it again. While she was sucking his dick, I noticed he closed his eyes and began to breathe like a bull. This was obviously turning him on even more.

Then he grabbed her, spun her around and slid his dick into her and began fucking her from behind. He was hitting her hard and fast. Like it was a race and he was trying to finish first. My wife was borderline roaring due to the intense pleasure brought on by his huge cock that was ramming her vagina numb.

I could hear him begin to groan louder and louder – as if something was building up inside of him. The groans continued and with each groan, it would get louder and louder. He puffed his chest up and then snatched his dick out before jerking her around and cumming all over her pretty little face.

By now, I knew I had to make a run for it before she came out and saw me. So I wasn't able to see the aftermath and what went down in fear of getting caught because getting caught was the absolute last thing I wanted.

So I left and went back home. Once again, I was all alone. I sat there for a while and my mind began to drift. I thought about all kinds of things. I reflected on life and our marriage. I wondered how this would affect our marriage because I knew I couldn't hide it forever. I began to wonder what my wife was doing at the current moment. I wondered who she was fucking. Was she with her boss? Was she still with Dan?

As the evening time approached, I still hadn't heard from my wife nor had she came home yet. So, like the sneaky little pervert that I am, I got bored and wanted to see her performing sex with another man. I left the house and decided to check out her office once again.

And so I pulled up, made my way inside into the elevator as it lifted me to her floor. The shimmery doors slid open and no surprise, I could hear my wife's low sounding moans reverberate throughout the floor. Like the night before, the lights were dim as well. Here we go, repeating the same events from the night before.

I tip toed over to her office, prepared to see her boss ramming her in the same position on top of the desk just as I did the night before.

I made it to her office door and peeked in but, to my surprise, not only was my wife's boss fucking her on top of the desk once again - in the doggie style position — but Dan was there as well, butt ass naked, sitting on top of the desk as my wife sucked his dick while her boss was fucking her from behind.

Now this was getting more and more bizarre each time I saw it. First she went from just fucking her boss - which was shocking — to fucking another dude the next day – which was even more shocking – to having a damn threesome with the same dudes the following night – which was totally shocking.

There my wife was, on all fours on top of a desk sucking away on another man's cock while another man kept plowing her from behind. I can't honestly say that this was getting out of hand, because it was really turning me on and I felt it kept getting better and better – for me at least.

I tried to stay in stealth mode and as quiet and chill as I possibly could. Who knows what would have happened if they caught me but I just could not turn away.

I watched as my wife's ass jiggled each time her boss' body clashed into her as he fucked her little pussy. I watched the pleasure on Dan's face as he groaned and moaned as she sucked away on his rock hard dick.

A moment or so passed and they – her boss and Dan – swapped positions. As they passed each other, they both slapped a "high five" like my wife was some trophy or something – which in my eyes she was, but to them, she was merely a piece of meat. Dan stood behind her while her boss sat down on top of her desk in front of her. She grabbed his cock like she owned it and began sucking away on it just as she was doing Dan's cock previously.

Dan – from behind- stuffed her pussy full of his dick and began fucking her fast and hard. She began to moan a little louder but tried her best to not go overboard with it. She was doing a great job at fighting it I must say. He was a lot quicker at fucking than her boss was and I'm sure she enjoyed his fucks a lot more so than she does her boss'.

Twenty or so minutes passed and finally Dan pulled out and came all over her face – just as he did earlier in the day. She then turned around and finished off her boss who eventually blew his load on her face on top of Dan's cum. They all relaxed a moment, catching their breath. She turned and I could see her face which was completely covered in cum belonging to two different men and I can honestly say it was like a work of art.

I decided to jet out before any of them spotted me. I made it back home and turned off all the lights before climbing in to bed. Again, I did not want to seem suspicious or act strange around her. Like the night before, when she finally got home, I pretended to be asleep as she tip toed in as quietly as possible, took a shower and then slipped in to bed and went to sleep.

The next day, I woke to discover my wife was gone once again. She slipped out on me without notifying me. But now, I officially knew why. So I texted her to find out what she was doing. It took a moment but she eventually texted me back to tell me she was working again. Of course, I wasn't shocked and I truly knew just what the hell she had been doing. So I sat around and thought about it a little while, wondering if I should take a break from watching her today. I figured to be safe I should, but the temptation of seeing my wife get fucked by other men was just far too strong. I had to do it and I couldn't stop myself. There was just something about seeing other men fuck my wife like a slutty prostitute that just turned me the hell on.

So I drove over to her office. I cruised around the parking lot to find her car and eventually did. Like before, I stepped out, entered the building, hopped onto the elevator and rode it up to her floor. Again, those familiar shimmery doors slid open and all I could hear was my wife moaning to the high heavens. This was unusual as the previous times she was attempting to not be as loud but there wasn't any trying today. She was screaming like it was the last time she would ever be fucked.

So I tip toed over to her office and peeked inside and my jaw dropped to the floor. Just when I thought it couldn't get any more bigger or epic than it already was, it did. Like I said, it seemed to get better each and every time and I am not bullshitting when I say that. When I peaked around the door, I saw not one, not two, not three but four men – four butt ass naked men, all surrounding my naked wife who was on top of her desk on all fours getting fucked in every orifice.

One guy - who I recognized as just a co worker – was fucking her in the ass. Dan was here again and he was on top fucking her in the pussy. Her boss was sitting on top of the other end of the desk with his dick inside of my wife's mouth. The last guy, who just so happened to be another co worker stood beside her as she stroked his cock. It was the literal definition of a gang bang and, although I had heard the stories, I had never seen one in person or on tv before. This was insanity – but it was a good insanity as I just stood back out of the way and enjoyed the show. This was better than any porno and I was seeing it live and in person and my wife was the star of the show. I don't even know how the hell she was managing this many guys but she damn sure was and she was handling them with ease – like a professional!

Throughout the fuck sessions, the guys would make jokes at my wife's expense and they were treating her like a real whore, but she didn't care. She just took their dicks like a champ.

Who was this lady because it sure as hell wasn't the woman I married? What the hell had gotten into her? Did she really have it that bad with me? Crossing the line was discovering she was fucking around with her boss, but this? Fucking around with multiple men at the same damn time just totally blew that line off the map. But as I've said, this was a sheer turn on for me and I just couldn't look away.

I watched as that juicy cock just slid in and out of her while she sucked on another. I watched as a big dick just penetrated her once virgin asshole (that had always been a virgin ass since we had been together – but not now). I watched as she used her right hand to stroke another cock. I could see the pleasure on these four men's faces and it was outstanding. What they were feeling – all courtesy of my naked ass slutty wife – could not be described in words. It was literally out of this world and you could just tell all by the looks on their smug faces.

My wife on the other hand? Oh, she was enjoying it just as much – if not more – as they were. There was an old saying, "If she had as many dicks going out of her as she did going in, she would be a porcupine" and that saying 100% applied to my wife today and was completely accurate and truthful.

I continued to watch from outside the door as the moans and groans grew louder and louder. It was intense, even for me – the viewer. It sounded as if they were all getting ready to climax and do it simultaneously.

Just as that was happening, it was then I felt a tap on the shoulder. It startled me for a second and my heart skipped a beat. I turned around to discover it was another man – who just so happened to be yet another coworker of hers that I recognized – standing there butt ass naked with a boner. I froze up a second, not knowing what to do. My cover had been blown and I didn't know if the guy recognized me or not. Hell, I couldn't even remember his name so hopefully he couldn't remember who I was.

"Are you here to fuck as well?" He asked. My lips quivered but formed no words. I stuttered, not being able to say what I wanted to say. He looked at me awkwardly, not knowing how to take it. It was then I noticed a strange silence. The group fuck that was taking place in the office beside me had ceased. Uh oh… I peeked into see my wife and all of the men she was fucking was staring a hole right at me. The funny thing was, they didn't look shocked or scared, they actually looked pissed.

Now I wanted to melt. My cover had been blown. How the hell was I going to dig myself out of this hole I kept thinking to myself. My wife looked at me with fire in her eyes – all sweaty and of course, completely and fully nude – and said, "What the fuck are you doing here?"

Of course, I was silent for a moment. I didn't know what to say. And then, just off the top of my head as my adrenaline was rushing, I simply said, "Just watching… and really liking what I see."

I think that threw everyone off guard – including myself. An awkward, tension filled silence really filled the air. That's when my wife jumped up, stared me in the eye with intensity and rushed over and got in my face. Like a real dominatrix, she groaned, "You like what you see? Yeah? You wanna see me finish them off? Huh? Is that what you want?"

Of course, I just stared in a trance and shook my head. My dick was growing and pounding in my pants. It made me want to whip it out and start jerking it off. That's how horny these people were making me.

She then gave me one last commanding look and said, "Fine. Watch me fuck the cum right out of their dicks." The she turned around, snapped her fingers and now all five men just swarmed her like a pack of rabid and feral wolves surrounding their prey. She jumped on all fours on top of the desk and bent over.

Then the dick went back inside of her pussy. Another dick went right back into her asshole. She grabbed another dick with her right hand. Then with her left hand, she grabbed the other dick. Lastly, she took the very last dick in her mouth and it once again became a huge gang bang. They were fucking her like wild and crazy men and it didn't take long. I knew that she was cumming based on her pleasure filled moan which was covered up with gargling and slurping sounds from the dick she had inside of her mouth.

Not long after, I don't know how she managed to do this to them all at once, but they all pulled out as she jumped down onto her knees on the ground and stuck her tongue out as they began jerking their dicks in front of her face. Each of the five men all began to cum and it just oozed down all over her face like slime. They were all moaning and groaning in pleasure as they unloaded their sperm all over her pretty little face. Her entire face was covered in cum. It almost looked as if she was hit in the face with a slimy pie. It was such a beautiful, artistic sight to behold.

And they finished up just like that. There I stood looking like a perverted porn addict and yet this was my fucking wife I was watching these five men do this to. In front of them, I didn't know how to feel but inside, I was feeling great. I wanted to run off and jerk off to what I had just witnessed. It was that great and by far the best acts of sex I had ever seen. It was a five star performance that deserved a serious round of applause from me and many, many awards.

So now, what was I supposed to do? It was time for me to come clean – even though my wife at the moment sure as hell wasn't clean. But perhaps now wasn't the time simply because her and I weren't alone. So I simply smiled like the little kind weakling that I was and left, ultimately deciding to have this big talk with her once we both got home.

I sat the house seemingly forever waiting for her to arrive. Finally, around midnight, she did. It was extremely awkward when she walked through the door but I had prepared everything I was going to say as soon as she entered. Of course, I froze up like the little cuckold bitch that I am.

She just stared at me. She was clean, believe it or not and dressed as if she was ready to go out, even though she was just coming in. I don't know what she did afterwards but I could only imagine.

"So…" is all she could say to me.

I then stood up and approached her, leaning against the counter. It was then I spilled the beans. I didn't know how she was going to take it or how she would react or just exactly what the hell she would do, but I did not hold back. I told her how turned on I was by seeing other men fuck her. I told her that I had been watching her secretly from the shadows. I told her about everything I saw. I completely opened up to her and emptied it all out.

She just smiled and to my surprise, she approved of it. She said if seeing other men fuck her turns me on, she could arrange to do it all the time. But now, she wouldn't have to do it in private or in other uncomfortable locations. Now she could get fucked by other men in the comfort of her own home. I agreed and now, I get to see other men fuck my wife all the time.

The Boat Is Rocking:
Does This Mean I'm A Cuckold?

It's been my wife and I for most of our adult lives. We got married at the early age of 19 and have been together for over ten years now. We were both happily in love when we got married and even to this day, we're both still happily in love.

Both myself and my wife are both 32 years of age. When we first got together at the age of 18 as seniors in high school, we were both virgins – or late bloomers as others would call it. Up until we had met each other, we had never had sex before in our lives. Unlike my wife when it comes to men, women simply do not find me attractive at all and I don't know what the hell my wife saw in me as I am ugly as sin. She, on the other hand is stunning and beautiful. I always said she is identical to Elizabeth Mitchell (from Lost) and looks like a younger and even more hotter version of her.

Even my friends and all of hers wonder what the hell she's doing with me because she's way out of my league but she loves me and I love her and that is truly all that matters at the end of the day.

I've lived with my wife for all of my adult life till now. We have lived with each other and all we have known for all of our adult lives up until now is each other. We've never had a fight and hardly ever even have disagreements.

With us spending every waking minute of our lives from the age of 18 until now, we still treated each day like it was our honeymoon and acted as if we were still hopelessly in love with one another. It's like nothing had ever changed. Many married couples grow apart and or flat out begin to hate each other's guts, but not us. We were unique and different. We were just as in love today as we were when we were teenagers in high school and that's the truth.

She scored a beach trip in Savannah, Georgia (a small beach town not in the Atlantic on the eastern side of the state of Georgia) to stay on an old-timing sail-boat. We weren't able to take it for a sail, but we were able to stay on it one weekend as all it basically served for now was a hotel. The only issue was it was a two roomed boat so there would be other guests on board – guests of whom were strangers that neither one of us knew. On our boat, there were two separate rooms – complete with a small bed (I don't know how you would describe it because it was so small, if you rolled over, you would fall off) and bathroom. The room's were small as well and additionally the rooms were on opposite ends of the boat. There was a door and a stairwell, which led down to each room (each room also had its own door as well). My wife and I both stayed in the room directly across from the room that was underneath the captain's quarters.

As we arrived, we met the guy we would be sharing the boat with. As I said, neither one of us knew who he was. He actually had two other guys tagging along with him as well. The main guy's name was Derrick. He was tall and handsome. Bald headed but young (possibly in his early 40s). Although he had his shirt on, I could tell he was in great shape and built like a bodybuilder.

The first day we were there, we were unpacking and getting a feel of our tiny but quaint little room. It was literally paradise!

As I came up from the stairs, I overheard a guy on our boat say, "She has a nice booty, doesn't she?" To which they agreed. I then heard him say, "I'm gonna try to hit that this weekend." They somewhat encouraged him.

I was shocked, but because I'm a sissy, I didn't want to say anything because I knew it would never happen. I heard him repeat, "Yep, I'm gonna see if I can hit it this weekend." Then he continued by saying, "If I can just get her away from that pussy- f'ing husband of hers long enough."

And that set me off. I charged up the stairs where they were standing. I wasn't going to do anything, but I didn't want to be a bitch. He saw me coming and his attitude changed instantly. He greeted me as if he liked me – just as he did when we met previously on board introducing ourselves. Normally I would've shaken my anger off, but I wasn't going to let it happen this time. I told him (this convo is not verbatim, but close to it), "I had better not ever hear you disrespect my wife like that ever again." He still acted nice by saying, "What do you mean?" I told him, "I heard what you said and I don't appreciate it." Then, he changed back to the bad ass he was originally by saying, "Oh yeah? What the fuck are you going to do about it, you little bitch?" (I then noticed my wife carrying a load of luggage from the car – which is what they were watching her do when he first said he wanted to hit her – but she wasn't paying us any mind). I was trembling in fear knowing I couldn't do a damn thing to this dude. So I politely said in response, "I don't want any trouble, sir. My wife and I simply want a peaceful weekend here and I would appreciate it if you just left her and myself alone." Mistakenly, that fueled his fire as he busted out laughing. Then he looked me square in the eye and said, "I hope you have a ton of money saved up because you need to prepare to pay alimony because that little bitch is about to leave you for a new mammoth dick."

As I said, I have lived with her since we were 18 years of age and when we got together, we were both virgins. My wife was one of the few girls who were actually good and had morals. She did not drink, curse or lie. She never has even spoke of another man as I was always the man of her dreams in her eyes (for whatever reason even I can't understand). In fact, she didn't even like watching R rated movies and half the time, PG-13 movies were too much for her. When we went out, it was to see an opera, orchestra, kid friendly movie or something similar. She always talked about the risk of STDs and never understood why people slept around – especially with others that they barely even knew. Trust me when I say the thought of my wife cheating on me never crossed my mind because she did not do stuff like that and I knew he had no chance with her. So he was basically wasting my time.

Back to the conversation, he kept on harassing and nagging me. I was clearly appalled by the disrespectful and tasteless things he was saying and comments he was making. I am not sure if he was trying to break me or what. I finally said, "Unlike you, my wife has morals and she isn't that kind of girl." He began to laugh and said, "That means I've already won and obviously I know your wife better than you do... and I don't even remember the bitch's name." His friends didn't really say anything.

He looked at me and said, "As I said, prepare to pay alimony because a new dick is going inside of her little pussy." I could not even speak as I was literally shaking. This guy was savage and flat out rude and intimidating.

As he walked off toward our very own room, my wife came up the stairs and they greeted each other smiling. I watched as they began to talk. Again, I didn't think anything of it so I let it slide.

Roughly an hour later, I was coming back to the boat (after eating) and noticed them standing on the docks, talking. I decided it was time to ruin this horrible man and approached them. As I drew closer, he looked and smiled and said, "Is that your husband?" She nodded and said, "That is him." But instead of talking to him, I walked right past without even acknowledging him. I didn't want to waste my breath on this idiot who was simply using her and playing Mr. Nice Guy simply for sex. My wife called out to me as I passed. I ignored her as well because I wanted to stay away from this jerk. I heard her say, "That is so rude!" But I kept walking. I did not want to get more crap stirred up nor did I want him to kick my ass in front of her making me look like a total cuck.

I didn't speak to my wife or Derrick for the rest of the evening because I didn't want to argue with him, and it disgusted me to see her talking to that idiot, and I tried to avoid it. I kept my distance. I ended up getting a text from her asking if I wanted to go out to get something to eat. I said yes of course. I met her back in the room and she told me that we were all going out – everyone – and that included Derrick and his gang as well. I stopped her dead in my tracks and said no. She asked me why I was acting so strange around him. Of course I could not say why but I simply said that I wanted to be alone tonight as I was not feeling very well. So she left and I did as well.

70

I decided to go have a few drinks at a nearby Tiki bar. The later it got and the fact that my wife hadn't texted or checked in on me me, I decided to return to the boat just to MAKE SURE everything was okay.

I walked down to my our room and she wasn't there, but her purse was. So I walked back up and walked toward the front of the boat to see her wrapped up in Derrick's arms and they were kissing. I was SHOCKED! But I didn't say anything. I stood there trying to plot a way to walk up to them, WITHOUT having him see me notice them kissing (because I know it wasn't sex, but I didn't want him to even have that). They broke away and hugged. With his head beside hers, he noticed me and smiled. He began to rub her back and then pointed at my wife's ass and mouthed what appeared to be him saying, "Mine". Then he stuck his tongue out and went back in for a kiss (though he placed the tongue back in his mouth before she noticed).

Obviously they weren't French kissing, so I could live with it.

I shouted, "What the hell are you guys doing?" They immediately broke it and looked at me is if they were both innocent. I told her again, "I can't believe you!" I could tell she was ashamed and didn't know what to say. He just said, "What is your problem?

Where I come from, this is what we believe. We kiss women as a thank you." I shouted, "Stop lying to me." My wife still remained silent and ashamed. I then dropped the bomb on her by saying, "He was saying very nasty things about you earlier and even called you a bitch." I tried to convince her of everything he was saying and doing, but he disputed it and she took his side. So I left, upset knowing he had kissed her – and even worse, she kissed him back.

I decided to stick around in our room, just to make sure nothing happened. I kept the stair and bedroom door opened (so I could hear if anything went wrong) as I was browsing my laptop, trying to get my mind off of the horrific thing I just saw. I began to hear SOME chatter upstairs. I snuck up to see them talking. They didn't say anything unordinary and he was acting fine. They then parted ways without kissing or even hugging. So maybe there was something more than I thought. Maybe it wasn't a big deal. She went downstairs to our room and he went downstairs to his. I couldn't help but breathe a sigh of relief knowing the kissing was all they had done but at this point, I was still nervous.

With him out of the picture now, I could go confront her face to face.

As she entered the room and closed the door, she stopped, staring me in the eye. I couldn't tell if she was scared, guilty or ashamed but I could tell something was up.

I immediately asked her, "What the hell was that? Over ten years of marriage and treating you like a queen literally bending over backwards for you and doing my best to give the world to you and you are kissing that asshole? Really?"

She then tried to defend him by saying he was a nice man who recently lost his wife and a bunch of other bullshit that I was not buying. He was an evil man who just wants to fuck my wife and ruin our marriage – that is who he was. She went on to say that she felt sorry for him and felt she had to kiss him. She said it meant nothing to her and she believes it was the alcohol that made her do it. So this idiot had her out drinking when she didn't even drink. In fact, she was anti-alcohol and had never taken a sip. I was shocked and pissed that this man was corrupting my innocent wife.

We ended up going to bed and not saying a word to each other. During the middle of the night, I could not sleep. I looked over at her to see her sleeping peacefully. I almost felt sorry about the entire predicament and felt perhaps she was right.

Maybe she really did feel sorry for him. Maybe it was the alcohol because it was not like her to do something like that. Now I felt bad about scolding her when she walked back into the room. There is no telling how ashamed the poor girl felt and I know she was only doing it to be nice because that is what kind of person she was.

The next morning I woke up to discover my wife wasn't in bed. I bolted up and searched the room, she wasn't anywhere in there with me. So I checked the bathroom and she wasn't in there either. I darted out of the room and ran up the stairs to discover she wasn't on the boat.

I looked to see that our car was gone as well. My mind was racing and my heart was beating rapidly. I called her and she did not answer. Now I was really a nervous wreck. About five minutes or so had passed and she called me back. I answered asking where she was and she told me that her and Derrick had decided to take a trip up the coast to a nearby beach. She said she had gotten up early and met up with him and they decided to go. She said she did not want to wake me up which is why she didn't tell me. I was pissed all over again and told her "I thought you were going to avoid him after the bullshit you guys did last night?" She calmly told me that was a mistake and it wouldn't happen again. I kept yelling at her and finally she asked why did I hate him so much. I told her why due to the fact that they were kissing and I know he wanted her. She assured me that wasn't the case. I ended up just flat out hanging the phone up on her because I did not want to hear this crap.

She was clearly brainwashed and more gullible than I thought she was.

I didn't see or talk to them for the rest of the day. Around sunset that evening, I ended up texting her to see if she was alright. Probably 15 minutes later (which was an unusual delay for her) I got a text back saying, "Yeah. Luv you."

Some more time had passed and I began to worry more and more about her, especially after knowing how long it took her to respond to my text and the fact that she was with him and had been drinking the night before and kissing him of all things. So I called, but couldn't get an answer. I texted her, "WHERE ARE YOU?" After a five minute wait, I didn't get a response. I texted the same thing again. Nothing. So I called again - and this time, I got an answer.

I heard her whisper, "ready?" I was thrown off guard, then I heard her saying, "Oh! Ohh! Ohhh!" I heard him grunt as well. I felt something wasn't right as they were doing so in a normal speaking voice and not very loudly as sex would be. I heard her say, "Oh, Derrick!" But it all sounded fake. I heard him say, "hang on," to which she silently moaned as if he was pulling out. He answered, "Hello?" And like a mad man, I shouted, "What the hell are you doing?" He said, "Who do you think?" But I could hear my wife laughing. I said, "Where the hell is my wife at?" And like a smart ass, he said, "Underneath me. Why?" I demanded he let me speak to her. Of course he then said, "She's a little busy but could really use a break. She sure needs one." I heard both of them laugh and when she answered, I let her have it!

Come to find out, they were eating at a restaurant and she put him up to it (even saying he didn't want to play like that– but that's what he wanted her to think). I asked where they were eating and she wouldn't tell me. I kept on and she told me not to worry about what she was doing and such. It's as if she was slowly turning and he was slowly turning her against me. I was very pissed and said to myself, "Okay! Two can play this freaking game!" So I jumped in the shower, cleaned up and put on the nicest clothes I had, which isn't saying much considering. I walked to a nearby bar and ordered a drink for the first time in a very long time. Like I said, my wife was anti-alcohol so I never drank around her. Actually, I had never drank while I was with her either.

At the bar, I decided to find a nice and attractive girl to talk to. Unfortunately, the majority of them already had men with them and these were men that put me to shame. They were handsome and I was ugly. They were built and in great shape and I was scrawny and weak. They were tall and I was short. So there was definitely no shot with them. I saw two women sitting a few stools down from me. They were attractive and did not have a ring on their finger – which did not matter to me at this point – and had no men around them or talking to them.

I approached them asking if I could buy them a drink and was quickly shot down. So I moved on to the next and was shot down. Then I moved on to the next and no surprise, was shot down. At this point I was pissed. I was pissed knowing my wife was out with a crazy man who was hell bent on fucking her and ruining our marriage. Meanwhile, my ass could not even get a girl to acknowledge me. So I tried one other girl. She not only rejected me, but tossed her drink in my face and told me I would never have a chance with her or any girl on the planet. So I was lit – lit as in pissed off to my limit. I said screw it and called my wife.

So I called, but could get no answer. Of course, I figured she wouldn't answer after what had happened earlier. I texted her telling her I was sorry and wanted to talk. I waited a little while, but got no response. Then, I began to get mad once again, thinking about him just being with her and her not talking to me because of it. So I started to blow her phone up. I kept calling and kept calling and kept calling. I swear I called about 20 times.

And then it happened.

A moment that almost changed my life. It caught me off guard at first because I was accustomed to hearing the ringtone. Then, I heard a real sound. It wasn't the fake quiet moaning from the restaurant.

It was a sound I will never forget and a sound I can't even begin to explain or mimic.

She was moaning so low and deep, it almost sounded manly. But it had a pattern to it as if she was moaning, "O-Uh-O-Uh-O-uh" really fast. It was something I had never heard out of her before.

I swear she never once stopped to catch her breath. I honestly didn't know how to react. I almost didn't believe it. Then, it's as if he placed her phone up to his mouth, he deeply said, "Oh yes… yes… that's good pussy." Then I heard the quick CLAPPING sound grow louder and louder as if he placed the phone down around where the action was happening. He was taunting me.

At first I thought they were joking again. But I knew as soon as he said, "pussy" she would tell him not to say that. But I thought maybe they were? Then I thought that sound was too real to be fake.

I was angry and sickened. Everything this man said about her. Everything he said he was going to do, she allowed it to happen.

Then it hit me: there's no way she would allow him to answer that phone if they really were doing it. It was around 10:30, so I went back to the boat, feeling better and better. But I WAS going to crawl her ass about playing around like that.

I noticed our car was there, so I felt almost like new. It was now around 11, and I knew she'd be in bed, but I was going to wake her up. I did not know where the hell Derrick was and did not care.

I remember opening the stairway door to our room and it hit me like oven heat. I heard that same moaning sound, but way louder. It was almost scary. The clapping sounded as if he was slapping a bare ass, but it was from their bodies smashing against each other. Their clothes were all over the stairs like they got started before they got to the bedroom. Shoes. Shirts. Bra and panties. Underwear. Socks. Pants.

Everywhere.

I considered even going through this assholes pants to see if I could find his wallet and possibly steal all of his money. At this point, it would be worth it because he should pay for what he is doing to me and ESPECIALLY for what he is currently doing to my beautiful wife. Then I figured once he found out any money whatsoever was missing, he would know it was me due to his pants being strowed out on the staircase and probably come after me and kill me. So I rejected the idea and moved on.

I walked down to see the door was wide open. I remember seeing them on the edge of the small bed. She was on her back and he was standing on the ground.

I just didn't know what to think seeing my sweet and innocent wife getting pounded like a prison slave — especially by this wicked piece of shit man who did not care about her and only wanted her for her pussy. I felt betrayed in a sense, and disgusted.

As disgusted as I was by the fact that this evil man who did not care about her and said some very nasty things about her, someway somehow seduced her, I was starting to get turned on by it. Seeing her getting screwed like it's the last night on Earth by a big, muscular and handsome man she barely even knew was somewhat of a turn on.

I remember when he laid over her, he would spread his legs out and I was able to see his big black nasty anus, before I could his penis. He was a white guy, but had a dark colored anal cavity and it was revolting. But I also noticed his penis as well. It was by far had the biggest penis I had ever seen in person. My wife's tiny little vag and surrounding area was blood red (and I wanted to vomit as I had never seen this region of my wife look as disgusting and beat out as it did here – if you ever see your wife's vag like this with another man inside of it, you'll feel sick as well). I remember it, and the entire region down there, being soaking wet as well. I don't know if it was sweat or her juice, but it was nasty.

He didn't have on a condom either and I couldn't help but think back to all those times she preached about other people having sex with strangers and not wearing a condom. Here she was with a guy on the second night BANGING him WITHOUT a condom. She had become one of the people she always complained about. This man turned her into a little whore who didn't give a shit about the potential sexual consequences of fucking a man she barely knew and had only recently met.

At one point he slowed down to a momentary stop. They were both panting heavily. I don't know how long they had gone before breaking (or even if they went non-stop the whole time), but as fast as he was moving, they needed a break. He would slowly stroke her and with each slow thrust, she would shout what sounded to be, "WHOA….. WHOA….. WHOA….. WHOA….. WHOA…" Though it wasn't as deep as the moaning, but it wasn't a clear "WHOA!" either. That's just what I could make of it.

Then, he stood upright and began drilling her really fast and the moaning ensued.

I noticed her cellphone was on the ground after I noticed her purse was beside them on the bed against the wall. All I could figure was as he was drilling her, he pulled the phone out and answered so I could hear and because she was in the throes of passion, she wouldn't notice – and she did not notice either. I have no clue why her purse was beside her yet her clothes were scattered everywhere in the hall (I can only assume she placed it there and they went out on the boat a minute before things heated up and they advanced down to her room).

At one point, he lifted her up. She sat in an upright position as he gripped her tightly while banging her hard. By doing this, I could finally see her face. She couldn't keep her eyes open as she rested her head on his shoulder. Her mouth was wide open and stayed that way as if it were stuck. Her left arm was tightly wrapped around his neck while her right arm was stretched out as if she was reaching for something. But it was just a reaction to a big hard dick being shoved inside of her tight little pussy.

I had never heard her make these noises before, nor would I have ever thought I'd see this. I also thought they had a lot of nerve to come onto THIS boat and in OUR bed to do it – especially her after how he acted around her behind her back. Here I am watching my wife make all kinds of crazy sexual noises that she never made with me. She acted like she was having a nonstop orgasm when I NEVER made her orgasm in all the years we had been together. This was truly a slap in the face and straight up demeaning and a huge blow to the ego – as if I had any ego to begin with.

This was the first time I had ever seen live sex before that did not include my sex of course. I was intrigued – so intrigued I wanted to see the ultimate climax. And not too long after, he slammed her down onto the bed and a few moments later, he pulled out (at least having the decency to do that) and jerked it until he jizzed all over the floor – and when he pulled out, his penis was bigger than I had originally thought – it almost looked fake. Neither of them said a word. For a second there (when he moved a bit to cum everywhere), I saw my wife's wiped out face and she wore a look I had never seen from her before. It appeared she had ran a marathon nonstop and had also just had a baby simultaneously. She was panting so heavy, it was almost worrying me. After he finished jizzing, he inserted his penis back into her and he laid on top of her. She wrapped her arms around him and rubbed his sweaty back.

Still, no words had been exchanged. They both panted and panted and panted. Then, with his cock still in her, he began to pound her while laying on her still, to which she yelled, "WHOA! WHOA! WHOA WHOA! WHOA! WHOA! WHOA! WHOA!" For

roughly about a minute and a half. Then he stopped.

I began to grow worried. I was thinking if they were done, I should bolt so they don't see me. I waited a moment to see if anything else happened.

So I quietly left and went to a nearby bar. I had a few more drinks and even tried my luck with a few more women. Of course, I had no luck as every single girl there that I even attempted to talk to immediately and instantly shut me down. As the time passed, I began to grow tired and bored – tired because it was late and exhausted from everything both my wife and Derrick had put me through throughout the day. I was bored from just sitting there alone and not having anyone to talk to.

So around two in the morning after the bar closed, I decided to sneak back over to our room to see if she was asleep. I opened the door and to my surprise, they were still going at it. Though she wasn't as loud as she was earlier, she was still moaning like crazy. I took a few steps down but noticed they weren't on the bed. I got closer and saw they were on the floor, doing it doggie style. They were completely drenched in sweat. He wasn't hitting her as hard as he was, but still hard enough to hurt her nonetheless. I recall seeing him grab what was left of my wife's blonde little pony tail at times, yanking her head up and holding it that way.

I could not help but wonder why the hell they were doing it in this room because they know I would eventually come back and catch them… or maybe that was the point? Whatever it was, I did not want them to know. So I quietly snuck over to the car got inside of the back seat, laid down and closed my eyes. Of course, my sick ass was so horny from what I saw, I just had to pull my pants down and jack off to seeing my innocent wife being fucked hard and wild by a bad ass man whom she barely knew and had only recently met.

The next day I woke up in the back seat of the car that I had fallen asleep in to a video text from my wife (of course it was from Derrick) that read, "mission accomplished" with a video of Derrick and her on the floor, doing it doggie style. It was a brief, 20 second video clip that was shot from his point of view. It was an upward angle looking down at her ass that was spread wide open and back with a big ass, monster cock ramming her once innocent vagina at light speed.

Now, it didn't really bother me as much at this point because it was over and done with. But I was still afraid to go outside, because I didn't want to face Derrick or even her. Plus, I knew I would feel weird toward my wife. I couldn't help but wonder what she might have thought or perhaps if she was having feelings of regret.

Knowing her, she was probably hating life right now and miserable. I am sure she woke up with serious regret and was probably feeling absolutely terrible about the serious mistake she made right now. In a sense, I almost felt sorry for her. At this point, I couldn't imagine how terrible she felt.

So I laid there a moment and gathered my courage not knowing what the hell I was going to do or say to her… or Derrick if I saw him. I did not want them to know that I knew about what happened. I figured they would wonder why I did not ever come back to the boat last night and would get suspicious. So I was simply going to say I made a friend at the bar, got too drunk to walk back and she offered to let me stay at her place, just so I wouldn't feel like a huge cuck and they would see that I can get someone else as well and play the same game as them. So I stepped out of the car and began the slow walk back to the boat.

As I drew closer, who do I see walking out and toward me? Derrick and my wife. The worst part was, there was obviously no regret on her part. She was not feeling bad even in the slightest about what she did last night. They were laughing and holding hands.

Then they both made eye contact with me. Even though I was walking, inside I froze. We drew closer and closer and my heart just beat faster and faster. It was seemingly endless.

Then, Derrick looked at me with a shit eating grin and said, "Do you remember what I told you? About alimony?" Then my wife looked at me and said, "I've called a lawyer. I am divorcing you, you bitch." Then they turned around and made out right in front of me. I could literally feel my heart melt. Then things began heating up between those two. He began to finger her as they continued making out. She began to moan, then he lifted her up and carried her right back down into our room, closing the door behind them. I just stood there as a few seconds passed and then I began to hear her moan with great pleasure.

So what was I to do now? She is divorcing me and is also with another man. How was I going to get home? Then the boat began to shake as if there were small waves coming through. I looked and the water was as calm as ever. Then it hit me: the boat is rocking due to those two fucking once again.

The Bully Becomes A Cuckold: Sex With Another Man's Wife

When I was in high school, I was terrorized by a guy named Brock Rutledge. Everyone seemingly had an assigned bully and he was mine. But he was more than just your average bully, he tormented me, going far beyond the normal stereotypical bullying limits. He gave me nightmares. He made me dread waking up in the morning. He made me fearful of going out in public outside of school. The last thing I wanted was to run into him. I absolutely hated going to school. As soon as I stepped off the bus, it was eight hours of non-stop horrific hell, each and every single day for four years.

I literally had PTSD from it. But in the end, he was the reason I was hell bent on changing my life.

The day after I graduated – and believe me, he made sure graduation was as miserable as it could possibly be for me – I began to change. I did not want to be the person I was in high school. I did not want to fear going out in public because of him. In fact, I did not want to fear anyone or anything.

So I began to work out. Every single day. No matter the conditions or how I felt, I would work out and I would give it my all. I began to change my fashion and look. Gone was the geeky long hair and clean shaven face. I changed my hair style to a number two fade. I grew out a slight beard. I started wearing slim fit dress shirts, stylish jeans and clean dress shoes. Gone were the days of super hero shirts, tacky baggy jeans and clown shoes. I began shaving my chest. I shaved my underarms. I always had a big cock, but I never could boast myself up to act like. Needless to say, I did not know how to use it either.

Day by day, my body began to change. I started devouring protein. The results were stunning and was only more motivation to keep going. I then found an affordable college that was a few hours from my hometown and graduated in a field I knew I would be successful in. I kept working out and began taking several different martial arts classes on the side while I was studying. I wanted to be able to kick someone's ass — specifically Brock's if I ever saw him again. By now, I was already in far better shape and more physical than he could ever dream of being.

While I was in college, girls were digging me for the first time in my life. Little did they know that just a few short years ago, I was the biggest loser in the world. Now I was the most desirable man on campus.

I finally lost my virginity. It was awkward and that wasn't enough for me. I began watching porn and studying books on sexual techniques and how to properly please a woman. The next girl who came along, I literally fucked her into submission. I had her cumming with my tongue and fingers alone. I could make a girl cum multiple times during oral and during intercourse. I couldn't tell you how many women I fucked on campus. I swear I fucked every girl in that town plus their mothers. It was a great time to be alive and I was no longer the gawky loser that I was in high school. I was now the the beastly hunk that every man wanted to be and every girl wanted in between her sheets. It was a major transformation that I am glad I underwent.

And I had Mr. Brock Rutledge himself to thank for that. But that wasn't enough. By now, I was no longer tormented by the horrific memories he gave me. I was pissed and I wanted to extract revenge.

Over ten years passed and by then, I landed a successful, six figure job in my hometown. I moved back and purchased a modest two story house and a brand spanking new BMW. I was in my early 30s and I was literally king. I felt like it and acted like it. But my goal was to find Brock and punk his bitch ass out in an even worse fashion than he used to do to me. I was out for blood and he was my primary and only target.

I went out each and every day when I wasn't at work searching for him. Whether it was a grocery store, restaurant, gas station, pub, club, you name it, I was on the hunt. But unfortunately, I never saw him. I did not have any friends from high school because no one wanted to be associated with me thanks to him. So I really and truthfully had no contacts from back then. I would see people whom I went to school with often out and about who I could tell did not recognize me from high school.

I started meeting and fucking women on the side, just for sport. I'd let them know from the get go that I wasn't interested in a relationship and only wanted one thing from them. Of course, they would always want more, even after I finished up with them, but I managed to push them away. After a while, I had given up on the hunt for Brock but on one particular Friday night, my luck would change and vengeance was nigh…

I was at the bar I usually hung out at. For a Friday night, the bar was surprisingly dead compared to how crowded and lively it usually is. A woman who was roughly my age came and set down beside me at the bar.

She gave me a look and then a smile. I could tell by the look that she was interested in me. Hell, at this point in my life, what woman wasn't? I could see it in her eyes that she was desperate. Something was going on in her personal life and she could use a nice huge dose of my big cock to lift her spirits.

I immediately struck up a conversation and discovered that she was having marital problems. She said she was sick and tired of her husband. She said he wouldn't work and she was the soul provider of all the household income. She said at times he would get angry and grab her. He never hit her, but he would get physically forceful with her. She said she wanted to leave him so bad but wanted more. She wanted to emotionally traumatize him on her way out. She wanted to leave on a high note.

And it was then she showed me a picture of him on her phone. It was Brock Mother Fucking Rutledge. I could not believe it. It was like the stars had aligned and I had the perfect way of extracting my revenge while helping his wife out in the process as well.

And so, I carelessly and shamelessly offered her a proposal, after spilling the beans that I hated him as well and wanted to torture him because he was a complete and utter jerk off in school. And so she listened as I offered to fuck her right in front of him and make his little punk ass watch.

I didn't know how she would react but I did not care. This was the perfect solution that benefited the both of us. And then, her dazzling blue eyes lit up like a Christmas tree and she smiled before accepting the deal.

So we both finished up our drinks and made for the door. She allowed me to ride with her as I did not want to take my new BMW over to their house.

Along the way, I thought about also kicking his ass. But I decided that getting physical with him wouldn't be necessary as this was the ultimate payback and there was no sense in violence – unless he tried to start shit with me and there was no way in hell he would do that now because he knows I could kick his ass.

And so we pulled into their driveway and all of the lights in the house were on. It was a nice suburban one story house. We plotted out our move and she decided she was going to go in first. She told me to wait until I saw the living room lights flicker on and off twice. Then move in and so I decided to do just that.

She stepped out of the car and walked inside as I sat there waiting and foaming at the mouth. All these years of hell that he inflicted upon me were about to be turned around back on him. I couldn't help but sit there with a huge smile on my face.

And then, I saw the living room light flicker on and off two different times. It was time for me to move in.

I stepped out of the car and approached the front door. All I could think about was all the shit he used to do to me and how I was just a mere few seconds away from royally paying his little bitch ass back. It was going to epic and monumental.

As I drew closer to the door, I could hear his voice asking, "What the hell are you doing, baby?" I almost cringed as I hated that goofy high pitched voice of his. His stupid voice alone made you want to straight up punch him in his little prick looking face.

I stepped up to the door and eagerly opened it. As soon as I stepped in, he turned around and we made eye contact. He didn't say anything and I knew he was trying to figure out who the hell I was and what the hell I was doing in his wife's house. And then, his face dropped. He finally figured out who I was and he stared at me as if he was staring at a ghost.

He couldn't speak. He was frozen. He was catatonic. He didn't look at me with that shit eating grin before getting in my face like he did in high school. He stood there knowing that I was now the bigger person and all those years of picking on me were about to blow up right in his once smug little face.

And so I approached him with me chest out and head raised high. His wife was standing over by the couch behind him watching. I got right in his face, eyed him up and down and I could tell he was intimidated. Hell he was borderline trembling.

I then grabbed him by the shoulder and said, "Come with me, you little dipshit." Little dipshit was what he always called me in school.

So, with my hand on his shoulder, I forced him over to a nearby recliner and threw him down in it. I then grabbed him by his shirt, bent over and got in his face, giving him the most evil, sinister look anyone had ever given him before. Then I said, "You are going to sit here and watch. You're going to watch what I do to your ex wife.

You're going to not make a sound. You won't make a peep. You won't move. Because if you do, I swear on your wife's little pussy that I am about to fuck, you will regret it. Do you understand me, you shit sucking little dipshit? Huh? Do you, bitch?"

All he could do is nod with wide, fearful eyes. I then let his shirt go and patted him on the back, telling him, "That's a good little dip-shit."

I looked over at his wife who was all smiles at this point. She was still standing before the couch, looking as sexy as ever — way more sexy than this piece of shit named Brock ever deserved.

And so I approached her and immediately put my arms around her. She was wearing a black dinner skirt. I began to make out with her and then I lifted her skirt up to get a look at what was underneath it and boy, oh boy, was I not disappointed. How the hell did this piece of shit land this is all I could ask myself. Her ass was so perfect and plump. It wasn't fat but wasn't small. It was just right and just the way it should be. No stretch marks or cellulites. It was firm and smooth, just like her body. Her skin was tanned but not overly dark where it's a turn off. She had it tanned to the point of perfection. Everything about this woman I was minutes away from fucking was perfect.

I turned her around where her ass was facing the little dipshit Brock along with my face. I was giving him the evil eye as I began feeling all over her ass. I was squeezing it hard and then I slapped it with force. He looked like a sad little puppy and I was enjoying every second of it.

I then went for the top of her dress and slid her shoulder straps down which caused her dress to fall to the floor. She had on a strapless bra and boy oh boy were her tits perfect. It was like the icing on the cake for a wonderful body – the type of body only a man could dream of.

I snatched her strap on bra right off and began to go to town on her tits. I bent down and started licking them, back and forth. One followed by the other. I could barely fit only the nipples in my mouth because her tits were that big. I then began squeezing them, giving them a nice massage that they deserved. Something his stupid ass probably never did. I was rubbing all over her tits and I could tell she was horny and that little pussy of hers was craving my huge cock. I then began to suck on her tits.

Again, one by one, I sucked them both, enjoying every second of it, unlike her little dipshit husband.

As I continued to rub and suck on her tits, I slid one hand down to her pussy. Keep in mind her thong was still on but I began rubbing her vagina. I was rubbing it gently, but this was the only time I was going to be gentle with her. She began to breathe loudly as she closed her eyes, enjoying what I was doing to her.

I kept doing so for a few more minutes and then I slid her thong off. I spun her around to get a full look at her nude and I can't emphasize enough how perfect her body was. She clearly worked out and was in great shape. No blemishes present on her body whatsoever.

I wanted to savor the moment for as long as I could so I began rubbing and feeling all over her body. Her neck, her hair, her face, her back, her torso, her tits, her pussy, her ass, her legs, I was feeling all over her. You name it and I was feeling on it. Her skin was so silky smooth, it was almost too good to be true.

I then stood up and began to remove my shirt. When she saw my body, her eyes widened and her mouth dropped. She stared in awe. I looked over at the little dipshit and he was doing the same. He could not believe my transformation and he knew I would destroy him if he tried any shit with me now.

She began rubbing all over my muscular chest and ripped abs. She bent over and began to kiss them. I allowed her to do it and then I grabbed her and placed her on her back over on the couch just beside the little dipshit so he could get a closeup view of what I was about to do to his wife.

I bent down and grabbed her legs, spreading them wide freaking open. Her pussy opened up like a rose blooming. It was beautiful, tight and pink — but not for long. I bent over and shoved my tongue right into her little pussy. It tasted amazing! As I was licking it out, I shoved two fingers right into her hole and began fingering her while eating her out. She began to move up and down, as if she was actually the one fucking me. She began to moan and breathe very loudly. It didn't take but about three minutes and she tightened up, gripping the couch as tight as she could and began to orgasm. That was orgasm number one.

I kept doing it and kept doing it for ten minutes until she climaxed once again, repeating the same motions and sounds. That was orgasm number two.

I leaned up and looked over at the little dipshit who was almost in tears. I held up two fingers and said, "Are you keeping count you little dipshit bitch? That is number 2."

Then I dived back into her pussy and continued.

I kept going until she hit orgasm number three. Once again, she repeated the same motions and sounds. This was number three. I looked back up to him and held up three fingers while giving him the most menacing stare that I possibly could.

By now, her pussy was soaking wet and craving my huge cock. I stood up and removed my pants followed by my boxers. When my dick popped out, her face dropped once again and I could see it in her eyes that she was hungry. Her little pussy was even hungrier. I looked over at the little dip shit and he was wearing a look of disbelief as he couldn't take his eyes off my dick. He could not believe that my dick was as big as it was. I know I was putting his ass to shame but there was absolutely nothing he could do.

She then leaned up and got off the couch. She dropped to her knees and began jerking my cock off before opening wide and swallowing it whole. She began sucking on my dick and it felt great. My face began tightening up as I looked over at the little dip shit, taunting him with my eyes. She was going to town on my dick and I was loving it. Factor in how humiliated the little dip shit was, this was the perfect fucking day. What a time to be alive and what a time for vengeance.

After a few more minutes of her blowing my dick passed, I then pulled away and laid down on the couch. She crawled on top of me and I spun her around in the 69 position. She once again swallowed my dick whole and began to suck it as I planted my face into her pussy and began licking it out.

We were going at it with our mouths and it was monumental.

We 69'd for about five minutes before I finally pulled her off of me. It was time. It was time for me to enter her little womanly cave with my huge manly rod. It was time to officially pay this little dip shit back for all the hell he had inflicted upon me for years.

I spun her around on all fours on top of the couch where she and I both were facing the little dip shit. Then I stood up and squatted down, grabbing my dick and entering her tight little pussy from behind. The sensation that washed over my body was amazing. Her pussy was so tight, so wet and so warm. It was just right! Right when I entered her, she let out a long, painful but pleasurable moan.

Before I began the epic fuck session, I looked over at the little dip shit one last time to see he was breathing heavily and look dazed – almost as if he was having a panic attack. I loved it. I gave him one last smile before I was ready to begin.

I then began to drop up and down as hard and as fast as I could, dropping my dick into her pussy like a bomb. She was screaming. At this point, she was way past moaning. She didn't even have it in her to moan. She couldn't moan if she tried because all that she could muster up was a scream. I was fucking her that hard and to her it felt that great. She was in another world – and it was the world of pleasure I was giving her.

I grabbed her by the back of the hair as I continued to pound her out from up high, dropping my dick inside of that pussy like a champ. I kept going, watching her body and ass vibrate like a wave each time my body clashed with hers. It was phenomenal!

I held on to her hair as tight as I could as I continued to drop those dick bombs into her pussy. Low and behold, her body began to tense up again. She let out a long and loud scream as her pussy clinched my dick as tight as it could. She then dropped her head and gripped the couch again as tight as she could and started cumming once again. That was number four.

As I was pounding her out, I looked over at little dipshit and said, "That is number four you little bitch ass dip shit!"

Bow! Bow! Bow! Bow! I kept dropping those dick bombs until it was time to switch positions.

I pulled out and dropped down on my knees. Then I entered her pussy from behind in the doggy style position and with all of my might and speed, I started tapping her from behind. I was going as fast as I could and as hard as I could. She began screaming again and it was less than a minute before she tensed up again, going through the same motions and sounds as I was making her cum yet again. That was number five.

I was pounding her out so fast and hard, I did not want to stop, even to taunt him. So instead, I simply held up five fingers and gave him another menacing look. Then I grabbed her ass as I kept going. I was lighting her little pussy up. Smack! Smack!

Smack! Smack! Smack! Smack! Smack! I was going hard, strong and at light speed. I was torturing this guy and I was also torturing her pussy. Needless to say, I was loving every second of it.

I kept going for a while before pulling out and flipping her over onto her back. Her eyes were closed as she was seemingly having an out of body experience. The sex I was giving her was that amazing!

I then spread her legs wide, placing them over my shoulders and then I – still on my knees mind you – slid my dick into her vagina and started going again. Once again, I was going as fast as I could and as hard as I could. Her body was shaking and the couch was moving all over the place. It was sliding back and forth while slamming into the wall. This was a masterpiece that not even porn stars could top.

I then shoved my finger into her pussy and began quickly massaging it while fucking the living hell out of her. Not even five seconds later, she slammed her hands into the couch, gripping it tight as her body tensed up, her head fell back into the couch as if she was bracing herself and then, she let out a long, drawn out scream as she began cumming once again. That was number 6.

I kept going as she was cumming and when she finally finished up, I noticed my dick was soaked. It was literally completely drenched in her pussy juice.

I went on for about five more minutes and then I pulled and dropped my face into her pussy and began to eat her out again. Her pussy was blood red, beaten out and soaking wet. It looked damaged compared to before I started fucking her. It was a night and day difference but I loved it and she was loving it as well.

I began to eat her out, licking all over her beat out little pussy before I took two fingers again and shoved them right into her little pussy. I started fingering her and eating her out simultaneously. It didn't take long before she once again repeated the same motions and sounds and started cumming again. I kept going until she was finished cumming. That was number 7. Number 8 was nigh…

I then leaned up and held up seven fingers at the little dip shit husband of hers and said, "That was number 7, you little dip shit bitch."

I then sat down on the couch, grabbed her and yanked her over on top of me. She spread her legs open and I then dropped her down onto my dick and began to force her up and down up and down up and down. I was forcing her to go as high as she could, all the way to the tip of my dick's head and then I dropped her right back down onto it. I was doing so fast and hard. She was riding it like a champ and taking it like a fucking champ as well.

Up and down, up and down, up and down on my long fat cock this little wife went. She was still screaming like she was in a horror movie, but this wasn't horror she was experiencing, instead it was sheer unadulterated sexual pleasure. And this was by far the best and most hardcore sex she had ever had – far superior than anything that needle dick little dip shit named Brock that she was married to ever gave her.

I then turned and laid flat on my back allowing her to continue her ride. She kept going and kept going and kept going and kept going until her body tensed up once again. She leaned back, stretching her tits and torso out. Her neck straigntened and eyes rolled into the back of her head as her hands gripped the couch. She began cumming once again. I started forcing my dick in and out as she could no longer ride it due to the intensity of the orgasm that was taking over her body. She was trembling and screaming to the top of her lungs.

This was number 8.

After she finished, I spun her around in the reverse cowgirl position, lifted her up a few inches and began to pound her out with no remorse. I was showing no signs of slowing down or stopping. My goal was to hit ten orgasms them blow a load all over her face, right in front of the little dip shit bitch that she was married to who made my life a living hell. I wanted him to see it all – and especially see the grand finale.

I was popping her hard and fast from underneath. Her pussy juice was splattering everywhere from my cock going in and out of her. Not only was her pussy and the surrounding area soaked, but my dick, balls and surrounding area was soaked as well. I did not give a single shit and neither did she. I was a machine and I was taking her ass down – right in front of her piece of shit little dip shit husband.

The couch was making all kinds of bizarre noises as it was moving across the floor and slamming into the wall behind it. Factor that in with the sound of my dick crushing her pussy, my body clashing against hers and her uncontrollable screams, it was an all out sexual concert. We were making sounds that her piece of crap, little dip shit husband would be haunted by for the rest of his miserable pathetic life.

I then leaned up, with my dick still inside of her and my torso touching her back. I reached around and grabbed her tits, squeezing them hard as she began to ride my dick up and down up and down up and down.

Shortly after, I pulled out, stood up and lifted her up onto the top of the couch. I sat her down while I stood before her. She spread her legs wide and I placed my hands against the wall to keep myself propped up. I then slid my dick back inside of her and went to town on that pussy once again. I was beating it out hard and fast. Bam! Boom! Bang! Slam! Clap! I kept going with full force and at full speed as well. She was still screaming and her voice had not gone out yet. It was still as fresh as it was when I first put my dick inside of her.

I stuck one finger back into her pussy. I could feel her orgasm brewing. It was building and building and building and building up. Then I felt pressure from her pussy and I pulled out. Just as I did, her body tensed up once again. Her eyes rolled into the back of her head as she screamed a long, never ending scream. She gripped the couch once again as tight as she could and stuck her legs straight out as she began to squirt all over the place. It was shooting out everywhere. About six squirts shot out. It landed all over the couch and floor beneath us. That was number 9 and I just had to take a second to gloat to that little dip shit of a husband of hers.

I looked to him with the most sinister smile and said, "I didn't know your wife was a squirter, little dip shit. I bet you didn't know that either, did you?" I then held up nine fingers as I stood there and continued by saying, "That is number nine, dip shit. Nine fucking orgasms. That is right, I've given your wife nine mother fucking orgasms, you little dip shit! Suck on that, prick."

I then slid my dick back inside of her, lifted her up into the air and started holding her as I began to power fuck her while standing. I was slamming her body hard into mine as my dick was pounding her once tight and innocent little pussy into pure ecstacy.

I was pounding her hard. Every smash was getting harder and harder. I could feel her pussy juice just splattering everywhere. And then, once again, she squeezed me really tight, buried her head into my shoulder, and gave me the tightest squeeze with her legs before she began screaming a long, never ending scream. Her pussy tightened up as I continued to pound her out and she began to cum once again. That was number 10.

I kept pounding her and pounding her and pounding her – throughout her orgasm and after it. I wasn't stopping either. While still holding her in the air, I turned to the little dip shit she was married to and gave him an absolutely wicked look before saying, "That is number 10 you pussy ass piece of shit little dip shit!"

I kept fucking and kept fucking, preparing to finally climax and cum all over her pretty little face myself. I had to build it up but it was coming.

I kept going and pounding her out via power fucking while holding her. I kept on and kept on and kept on. I was focusing on the grand prize. I was focusing on busting the nut. It was brewing and I could feel it building up. I squeezed her tighter as I kept clashing her body into mine. She was still screaming like there was no tomorrow. I began to growl. I was focused. I was a predator feasting on the prey. My dick was the actual predator and her pussy was the actual prey. My goal was to explode all over her pretty little face and I was working extremely hard to accomplish that goal.

I looked over at her little dip shit of a pussy ass husband to see he was setting there catatonic. It was as if his wife and I had fucked so hard, he was a zombie. Shock had taken over his pathetic little body and now it was all a daze. But it wasn't a daze. It was a reality – and the reality was his wife was right in front of him getting fucked and fucked hard at that by another man – another man whom he tortured all throughout high school. And now this man who was once a huge dork and loser was now paying him back in the most humiliating fashion. This man was fucking the living hell out of his wife's pussy.

My dick began to tingle. I could feel the cum shooting through my slong. I was getting ready to explode. So I pulled out and dropped her onto her feet. I stepped off the couch and motioned for her to step off as well. By the look in her dazed eyes and fatigued face, she knew what was about to happen. She stepped off the couch and immediately dropped to her knees. I stood before her and placed my long ass, rock hard and fat dick right in her pretty little face. She opened her mouth as wide as she possibly could and stuck her tongue out. I used her wide opened mouth as the target as I began to jack off hard and as fast as I could, aiming the tip of my dick right at her mouth. As I said, her mouth was the target and I was aiming directly at it. My goal was to nail the target and I was working as hard as I could to accomplish that goal.

I could feel it coming. It was close… closer… closer… closer… and then… cum began shooting out like missiles, nailing her right in her mouth. The first two shots landed in her mouth and then I aimed for her face and began cumming all over. Cum was flying out everywhere like bullets and nailing her in the face, splattering all over it. It was glorious. I began making sounds to taunt her little dip shit bitch of a husband over in the chair watching.

I was groaning loudly as I kept unloading and unleashing my sperm all over his wife's pretty little face. By the time I was done after the last little drip nailed her in her pointy little nose, I looked down to see her entire face was washed in my sperm – my fucking bodily fluids.

When she saw that I was done, she fell back over onto the couch on her back. She couldn't move. She was exhausted and completely worn out – both physically and sexually. Her pussy was destroyed and it was all because of me.

She was covered from head to toe in sweat – and it was then I noticed that I was as well. She wasn't bothering to wipe the cum off of her face. She just laid there and allowed it to remain on her pretty face.

With my monstrous dick still hard and throbbing, I walked over to the little dip shit, bent down on one knee to get eye level with him and grabbed him by the shirt, pulling him face to face with me. I then gave him a cold hard stare in the eyes and said, "Your wife wants a divorce. And she wants to keep fucking me. So why don't you get the fuck out before I do to you all the things you used to do to me, you little dip shit bitch."

He then fearfully nodded with a tear in his eyes and said, "Yes, sir. I am sorry for everything I ever did to you. I am so sorry."

I smiled sinisterly before saying, "Get the fuck out. And I better not ever see you again. You better never cross my path. You better refrain from going out in public. This isn't a warning either. Get the fuck out. NOW!"

Just like that, he shot up and darted out of the living room, fleeing the house in a hurry.

I then looked to his exhausted ex wife and said, "Are you ready for round two?" She leaned up with a big smile across her cum stained face and said, "Bring it!"

The Poor Cuckold:
A Stranger Makes My Wife Squirt As I Watch

My wife and I had just left the mall and were walking through the parking lot towards our car.

We were both carrying loads of bags which contained clothes, blu rays, etc. I was already upset at the amount of money my wife had spent as finances had been tight here of late.

My wife was laid off from her job over six months ago while I was struggling to make provide for the two of us. I was solely responsible for our income and money was very tight, yet she just wasted a ton of it on useless stuff. If an unfortunate incident occurred that required a lot of money to be fixed or repaired, we would be in serious trouble.

Of course, tensions were high between us and she was just as stressed as I was. She took great pride in her job and being laid off was a real blow to her pride. She had taken a lot of it out on me through verbal abuse and of course, today, she took a lot of her stress out on shopping and blowing money that we did not have to blow.

My wife and I have been married for almost two and a half years and she is still as gorgeous and sexy today as she was the day we first met. People always said she was way out of my league and believe me when I say they are not lying when they say that either. She is still a perfect ten and absolutely drop dead gorgeous!

I was in a foul mood because I knew how much she had spent while she was pissed at me simply for being pissed. Of course, this was nothing new as she has been in a foul mood for a long time and basically always takes it out on me.

Throughout the walk to the car, we did not say a word to one another nor did we even bother giving each other a look. We acted as if the other was not present. We were not walking in tandem, we were not holding hands and we were not even bothering to acknowledge one another. We were both on our own personal mission to the car and we were doing so alone, just conveniently at the same time basically.

When we arrived at the car, I popped the trunk without saying a word to her and she of course did not say a word to me either. I dropped the bags into the trunk and she dropped her bags in there as well. I did not even bother closing it for her. I just got into the car and left her with that duty. Now I am usually a gentleman, but not so much today or here of late either due to the mood she stays in. I always say it is best to avoid her when she is like this.

After she closed the trunk, she stepped in as well and threw her ear buds in to avoid talking to me. I continued to ignore her as well, acting as if she wasn't even there.

I started the car and let the AC run a second to cool things off before I backed out. Then, I put the car in reverse and started backing out.

All of a sudden, we heard a crash and were jerked around for a bit. That is when I realized I backed out in front of someone. This couldn't possibly come at a worse time!

She immediately started screaming at me, calling me names, reminding me of the consequences of what just happened. Of course, it was one of those things you couldn't help. Two cars on both sides were blocking my view so I had no way of seeing who was coming and who wasn't. It was a 50/50 shot and luck wasn't on my side on this day. Little did I know…

So I had to take a deep breath. I had to try to relax. It was hard to concentrate and focus over the sound of her screaming bloody murder and verbally insulting me. My nerves were shot and I was shaking as my anxiety was brewing. I had no money right now and I knew my car insurance was going to skyrocket because of this. I could barely afford to pay my car insurance now and even a dollar increase would put me in the hole. That is how strapped for cash we were.

A few seconds passed and all of a sudden, there was a knock at my window. I turned to see a buff body builder throwing his hands up. Great! This couldn't possibly get any better, could it?

I knew he was either going to kick my ass physically or have his insurance company kick my bank account's ass. All I could do is roll my window down and prepare for the worst. And I did just that.

He stuck his head through the window with an angry look on his face and said, "What the fuck are you thinking, guy?"

"I am truly sorry," is all I could muster up.

"You are gonna be!" he said before he strangely noticed my wife sitting there. His eyes focused on her and were instantly locked. I noticed this and turned to her to see that her eyes were locked on him as well. Neither one of them were blinking and she was giving him a look I hadn't seen her wear in years. It was as if all of that stress had finally worn off.

"Who is this?" He asked.

Before I could even tell him her name, she said it for me, reached over me and shook his hand. I could see a chemistry was brewing between the two and it was awkward for me. I just sat there like a third wheel while my own wife lustily stared down another man.

"You're one gorgeous woman" he said to her. She replied, "And you're one hunk of a stud."

Once again, there I sat not knowing what to say or do. So I tried to interject by saying, "Look sir, my wife and I are both having financial difficulties…"

Then, the unthinkable happened. He interrupted me and said, "Tell you what, why don't you two follow me to my house and we can work something out. I want your wife. I will fuck her and in return, I won't fuck your little puny ass up."

I was stunned. I was speechless. My lips quivered but formed no words. Before I could even say anything, she screamed, "Deal!" And then stepped out of the car. He then looked at me with menacing eyes and commanded me to follow him. All I could do was obey his commands because I couldn't afford not to.

So they hopped in the truck together and I simply followed behind. His windows were tinted so I could not see what was going on but it had me curious. What were they doing – if anything? Were they kissing along the way? Was he feeling all over her? Was she feeling all over him? Was she showing off any cleavage to him? Was he showing her his junk? Was he fingering her? Was she giving him a hand job as he drove? Was she giving him a blow job? All of these thoughts were racing rapidly through my mind. I just knew something had to be going on, right? The butterflies in my stomach were growing just thinking about it and thinking about what was going to happen – right in front of me before my very eyes – whenever we got to his house.

The drive was a bit longer than I had originally anticipated. He lived almost 30 minutes away from the mall so needless to say I had a lot of crazy thoughts going through my mind that I could not block.

We ended up pulling into a modest, upscale neighborhood. It was gated, clean and luxurious. It was way nicer and fancier than the dump we lived in. This guy had everything going for him compared to me.

And so I followed him into the driveway of a three story home that was tucked away from the rest of the houses. They could literally fuck outside and no one would see or probably even hear them. My wife wasn't a screamer after all anyway.

And so we stopped in the driveway. I parked behind him. His driver door opened but strangely, her door never opened. Then he stepped out, carrying my wife's body over his shoulder with ease. She had a big smile on her face while he stood there with that menacing stare. He looked at me with the most intimidating, alpha male stare and motioned for me to follow.

I got out of my car and followed them to the front door and into the house.

The house was clean and fancy. I never would have thought someone like him would live in a house so clean and nice.

As soon as we stepped in the door, he dropped my wife and they began making out right in front of me. His hands were rubbing every inch of her body while her hands felt all over his muscular chest that put my little bird chest and ant bite boos to shame.

Things were heating up fast and they didn't even have their clothes off yet. I did not know what to do or how to react. So I just stood there as quiet as I could possibly be. If anything, all I could think about is one fuck up on my part and this guy would kick my ass and still report the wreck and that is something I couldn't afford. So I was going to stand here and observe while offering up my innocent wife as a sacrifice to this burly he-man.

I watched as he began to squeeze her boobs very hard. Then, in one quick motion, he snatched her shirt off, squeezed her tits once again and then snatched her bra off. He dove his face into her tits and began sucking them like there was no tomorrow. He was sucking them with force and squeezing them to their limit. Any harder and he would have popped them. Then, by grabbing her boobs, he yanked her over toward him, shoved his tongue in her mouth and removed his shirt in the process.

His body was phenomenal. He was huge and had muscles on top of muscles on top of muscles on top of muscled. Literally. The guy was a walking barbell.

My wife's jaw dropped and her eyes widened in sheer eagerness. She loved his body and was craving it. She slowly began to feel all over his burly chest in a mesmerized state. While she was doing that, he reached down and pulled her pants down leaving her g- string on. He began rubbing all over her thighs and ass. Then he spun her around, bent over and began to grab and squeeze her ass. He started licking both of her cheeks before he spun her back around and yanked her g-string off.

"That is a pretty fucking pussy you got there," he said to her.

She simply replied, "Thank you" with a smile.

He then pointed his middle finger at me and then shoved that same middle finger right into her pussy. I saw my wife's eyes roll into the top of her head as he started fingering her hard and fast. It was like a jackhammer going in and out of her tight little pink and innocent pussy. She was moaning bloody murder and her entire body was shivering.

He then pulled his finger out and shoved it into her mouth, making her suck her own pussy juice off of his middle finger. He then looked at me and gave me the most sinister look before pulling his pants down revealing a long, huge, throbbing and muscular looking dick. It was the biggest dick I had ever seen in person and on the pornos I watch late at night. It was massive and incredible. It was a literal sight to behold that you had to see to believe.

My wife felt the same way. Her mouth opened wide in shock and her eyes were bulging. She couldn't believe it either. She was awestruck and speechless. She tried to say something but couldn't. She was too caught up in the moment and shocked by seeing a fairy tale dick.

He grabbed my wife's head and forced her down to his dick. Then he shoved it into her mouth and began to hump her face. I could not believe it but she was taking every inch of this monstrous dick. All the way down. Her eyes were watering as the pressure was from his thrusts were overpowering her. Then he pulled that massive dick out, spun her around, grabbed both of her legs, lifted her up, forcing her to do a hand stand and then he shoved his tongue right into her asshole. She began to moan and breathe hard as he licked her asshole clean.

Then he took that same tongue and shoved it into her pussy. Her body once again began to tremble as her arms were growing weak. She couldn't take it. She was moaning like I have never heard her moan before. She began to walk with her hands and he followed, keeping his tongue stuck to her pussy. I tagged behind as she walked – using only her hands – all the way over to the staircase, propping herself up a little higher. He then began to bounce up and down as if he was already fucking her.

He kept doing this for about five more minutes and then stopped. He laid down on the staircase, grabbed her with power, spun her around with her ass over his face and then dropped her pussy down onto his tongue while her face landed on his dick. They began to 69 on the staircase and it was gruesome. The sounds of her moaning combined with the sounds of his groaning and the intense licking and sucking sounds was something borderline unheard of. They were all echoing throughout the house and it was loud. It was spine tingling and haunting. If there were neighbors around, they would DEFINITELY hear them!

He rolled her over onto her side as they both laid there on their sides 69'ing. He then hiked one of his legs up in the air – I suppose so I could get a better look at her sucking his dick – and kept it hanging as she sucked his dick like a champion. It was humiliating because she NEVER sucked my dick as passionately as she was sucking his massive, deformed looking cock. She was hungry for it and taking that bad boy in her mouth like a champ!

A few more minutes passed before he finally pulled away and laid on his back. Then he grabbed her by the ass, spun her around facing me. She spread her legs wide across his legs, grabbed each hand rail with her hands and hovered her pussy above his monstrous cock.

I could see her face. By the hungry look, she was craving his cock to go inside of her pussy. He grabbed his huge cock and started forcing it into her tight little pink pussy. It took a few seconds for her vagina to completely swallow it but when it did, that was it. He finally had it all the way in and her mouth opened wide as the pain of this huge cock entering her pussy was too much for her to handle – but she was handling it with ease.

So there I stood, watching as my wife took another man's dick – and a huge dick on top of that. A man she didn't even know. A man whose name she didn't even know. A man she met a little over thirty minutes ago. My wife who swore to remain committed to me broke that promise in the snap of a finger.

As his dick entered her completely, she let out a deep, guttural moan. It was scary and deep. It's like she was possessed. And that was it…

He began to pound her pussy hard and deep, slamming it with full force like he was working out with weights. It was powerful and loud. The smacking sound of his body clashing against her little body was deafening. And to top it off, she was moaning like I've never heard her moan before.

He was pounding away as I could see her pussy juice just splashing everywhere from her once little tiny pussy that was split wide fucking open by this beast of a cock that this powerful and muscular man had. It looked sick and disgusting. Almost like she was giving birth to his cock and it was trying to go back up inside of her. It was like a fight.

He then stopped on a dime and stood up, with his dick still inside of her. They were still standing on the steps and he was a few steps above her. In a standing doggy style position, he began to pound her out again. Her head slumped down where I couldn't see her face but I know it revealed a feeling of full blown ecstasy. Based on the weird moaning sounds she was making, there was absolutely no doubt about that.

I looked up at him to see him giving me an evil stare. Looking me right in the eyes as he fucked the living hell out of my wife.

Then, after about five minutes or so, he yanked his cock out, spun her around, shoved his tongue in her mouth again, then grabbed her by the legs, spread them wide fucking open, lifted her up into the air and dropped her pussy down onto his hard cock that was sticking out like a log. He started power fucking her while holding her. He kept on and kept on and kept on as it kept growing more and more intense by the second. He was fucking her hard and fast. It was insane!

Then he motioned for me to follow him as he started walking, while still holding AND fucking her. He was using his arms to clash her pussy into his dick. And he was walking on top of that. This man was gifted and talented. He was a true sexual multi tasker and I could only imagine what was going on inside of my wife's head... of course, I know what was going on and she was blank. She was on a euphoric high of having all of her brain cells fucked right out of her. She probably did not even know her name at the moment. He was fucking her dumb. Literally.

So I followed him into the kitchen, which was nice, fancy and rather spacious. He walked over to the kitchen table and sat her down, while he still stood up and kept his huge cock inside of her. Then he began pounding her out hard, powerful and fast. The table was rocking and I expected it to break any second. As hard as he was fucking her, I was surprised the legs on the table never gave. It was like a fucking earthquake.

My wife wrapped her arms around his muscular upper body and squeezed him tight as he gave her the ride of her life. She planted her head into his chest as it muffled the sound of her loud and intense moans.

He kept on going and in the process, he grabbed her by the back of the hair, yanked her head back, stared her in her half shut eyes for a minute as he continued to fuck the shit out of her. Then he stuck his tongue out and shoved it back into her mouth.

I could see his firm and ripped up ass just flexing with each thrust. He was an amazing specimen and as unlucky as I was, I couldn't help but think from my wife's perspective, she had to have been the luckiest girl on planet earth right now.

A few more minutes passed before he grabbed her by the legs again while leaving his dick inside of her and lifted her up into the air again. Once again, he started power fucking her while standing and holding her. He looked to me again with his evil eyes and motioned for me to follow him while he carried her, fucking her in the process. This man was a machine and there was no way in hell anyone in this universe could ever top this dude. He was simply put: phenomenal.

And so I followed him into the living room where he had two huge wrap around couches laid out and a recliner. While still holding her with his dick inside of her, he sat down on the couch, snapped his fingers at me and motioned for me to take a seat in the recliner that was facing them. I did just that and watched as he began to fuck her while sitting there. He was fucking her so hard, the couch started moving back, out of place. But neither one of them gave a shit.

Then, with his dick still inside of her, he flipped her around, reverse cowgirl style and she was facing me. Then he began to fuck her fast and hard in that position.

This guy was a machine and wasn't slowing down or showing any signs of slowing down either. He continued to impress me the more I watched him fuck my wife into submission.

A few minutes passed before he grew bored and actually stood up, holding my wife while keeping her in the same position. His dick was still inside of her as they both faced me, with her back to his stomach. He was holding her legs and had them split wide open. Then he walked over toward me and got as close as he could while putting her pussy that was split wide open from his huge dick in my face. He then began to fuck her just inches away from my face. I could see it all in great detail. His vein covered, huge dick that was soaking wet from her moist vagina stretched her once tight little pussy to its max. It was blood red and was soaked. That entire region of her body was soaked.

My wife began moaning a weird sound. Even weirder than before. It was as if something was brewing inside of her. The sound kept building until he stepped back, snatched his dick out and she squirted all over the place. Squirt! Squirt!

Squuuuuiiiiiiiiiirt! Squirt! Squirt! It was endless and she would scream bloody murder with each squirt. There was a massive puddle on the ground beneath them from all the fluids she just released. The entire time she was squirting, he kept saying in a low, deep and horny tone: "Oh, yes, baby. Yes! Yes! Yes!"

Then her body tightened up and was completely stiff. He was still holding her in the air, mind you, and then as soon as she finished, he planted his monstrous dick right back inside of her and picked up where he left off. It was like there was no delay. He started fucking her hard and fast and she went back to her usual moaning that was eerily creepy.

He walked over to his patio door and planted her face into it while dropping her feet to the ground. He stood there fucking her from behind while the door rattled like a hurricane was rolling through. It was loud, fast and intense.

She was doing her best to grip the door but it was a losing battle. The sound of his body clashing into her ass was epic!

Her face was planted into the door and muffling her moans but that didn't stop her or slow him down. He kept going and fucking her hard and fast, like a fucking bull on cocaine.

It almost felt like the whole house was shaking just by her body slamming into the door and the deafening moaning sound she was making. Factor in the hard smacks against her body courtesy of his, it was almost like a mini earthquake.

He finally slung his arms in between her arms and forced her to back away from the door. With his dick still inside of her, in the same position, they started slowly walking back toward me. About halfway through, he stopped and just started pounding her out right where they stood. She immediately started screaming again as he was driving her pussy hard and fast. Once again, after all this time and hardcore fucking, neither one of them were showing any signs of slowing down or stopping. As I have said before and I'll say it again, this still beats having to pay money that we absolutely cannot afford to shell out, so all I could do was sit back and continue to enjoy the show.

He kept going and going and going as they stood there with his arms wrapped around hers as she stood upright, just like him with her back to him. Then, she started making that weird moan again — like something inside of her was brewing. I knew what that sound was: her little pussy was getting ready to squirt again. They were maybe 5 feet away from the last spot she squirted in and that puddle was still fresh.

Then, just like that, he snatched his dick out and her body began to tremble as she squirted all over the ground beneath her. It was exactly like the last time she squirted. The pattern of the squirts. The sounds she made, it was all identical. Me, I was never able to make my wife cum or squirt – hell, I did not even know she was a squirter! And yet, this dude, within 15 minutes or so, had her squirting not once, but twice. That should tell you all you need to know about how fucking amazing he was.

After she finished up, he laid down in that very puddle and began to roll around in it like a pig in the freaking mud. It was disgusting and he was obviously a freak. Then he leaned up, grabbed her by the arms, spun her around doing a complete 180, grabbed her ass and snatched her down to the ground, reverse cowgirl style again, and slammed her pussy down onto his cock. Then he began to beat her tight little pussy out in this position.

They kept going on and on and on and on and finally, he stood up, grabbed her legs, spread them wide and lifted her up once again into the air, sliding her pussy down onto his cock. He began to power fuck her in the air once again for a few minutes.

Then he looked at me with those familiar evil and eyes and said in a commanding and alpha voice, "Get your fucking ass up!" Like the little bitch that I am, I stood right up and moved out of his way. While still carrying her, he walked over to the recliner I was just sitting in, sat down in it – with his dick still inside of her, mind you – then kicked back and began to rock it violently back and forth as he fucked her harder and faster than he did the entire day. This guy had been going at it a while now and was now fucking her even faster and harder than before. There was no quit in this guy. He was a physical freak of nature and a champion at that!

He kept pounding and pounding and pounding while she screamed her lungs out. I just knew that eventually her voice was going to give.

Finally and without warning, he snatched his dick out, stood up while forcing her to the ground, shoved his cock in between her two little perfect perky titties and began to titty fuck her once again hard and fast. He was groaning and moaning as if he was ready to explode all over her.

He kept going fast and hard without slowing down. He was

picking up speed, going faster and faster. I started thinking her poor little titties were going to have road rash from the friction of his huge and violent dick that was showing her absolutely no mercy whatsoever. I was thinking about the road rash his massive and monstrous cock was going to receive as well but he did not care and clearly showed it here. He wanted to make this fuck worthwhile and believe me, I know that from my wife's perspective, he definitely was.

He began to yell very viciously. He was a mad man who was growing more and more sexually psychotic by the second. He was squeezing her boobs to their limit while literally fucking her tits with his huge dick going 90 miles per hour seemingly. He was out of control but she loved it and so did he.

Finally, he made a grunting noise as his massive dick slid out from her blood red tits and then he shoved his dick inside of her mouth and began to hump her mouth once again. His entire dick was going into her mouth and down her throat and she was having zero issues taking this huge dick in her mouth, which was impressive to say the least. His super muscular ass cheeks began to clinch up. He groaned and grunted louder and louder, then he began to moan in pleasure as he jizzed all inside of my wife's mouth. He looked up to the ceiling with his eyes closed as he just dumped his entire load into my wife's once precious and innocent mouth that was now forever tainted by his huge dick, body funk and his sperm.

He kept on jizzing until the final load was dumped. Her eyes were watery and opened as wide as they could go. Then he snatched his dick out while breathing heavily. When he pulled it out, there was slime still connecting from his dick to her mouth. He snatched it away and did not even bother to look at her again. Then he turned to me and said, "We are even now. Get the fuck out of my house."

I looked to my wife, who was suffering from post traumatic fuck syndrome and smiled a big smile of relief. He walked away, out of sight and we never saw him again. I had to go round up her clothes, which were all over the place. Then I had to basically help dress her because she was out of it. She was physically and mentally drained from the intense fuck and mind blowing orgasms she received.

We exited the house and just like that, I didn't have to worry about forking over any money to this man or my insurance company. We left in my car together and never spoke a word about this incident to anyone else or each other ever again.

Anniversary Hotwife:
Watching My Wife Get Split Open By A Giant Cock

His dick was the size of a banana. Literally. It was the biggest – both in girth and length – dick I had ever laid eyes on. Here I sat Indian style in only my boxers on the floor directly across from my wife and her new lover.

This practice was an annual tradition for the two of us. Each year for her birthday, she finds a new man to fuck right in front of me while I'm required to sit, watch and enjoy.

This year, she wanted this tradition to be extra special. In the past, she's gotten with semi-decent men – even a few women – but if they weren't lacking in the experience department, they were definitely lacking in the size department and vice versa. Due to never being able to find the perfect man to fuck for this special occasion, she decided to do a little extra research this year while placing more effort into the search department. Instead of searching within the limits of our city, she expanded the search nation wide. Eventually, she found a man from Los Angeles, California who had the look, body, dick size and sexual experience she so desired. He had done quite a few pornos and was even a "juggalo" who was paid to service unhappy wives and mature women who couldn't quite find the right guy. As far as cuckolding was concerned, he did that as well. In fact, he said it was his favorite. He told my wife straight up, "Nothing gives me more pleasure than to fuck a horny wife senseless right in front of her helpless husband." His name was Big John and that was it. No real name. No last name. Nothing. Zilch. All we knew him by was Big John – and believe me when I said he certainly lived up to that name.

Just like that, he was hired and as a birthday gift, I paid for his travel, hourly fees and hotel expenses. This was going to be the greatest gift ever for the both of us. Hell, even Big John himself would consider this a great gift as well. Without a doubt, he most certainly would because my wife was a certified hottie. She worked out 24/7 to maintain a model-like body. Literally, she could work a runway if she wanted too. Both her face and her body was a perfect ten. She had long black hair, piercing blue eyes and again, a body that could put any woman to shame. She was the perfect woman and here she was offering herself to this stud simply known as Big John.

Truthfully, they were more perfect and compatible for each other than she and I were. But who cares? This was a tradition and all three of us were bound to enjoy it.

They both stood there butt ass naked, making out and shoving their tongues down each other's throats, swapping spit and god knows what else. I simply sat and watched as my dick was growing harder and harder by the second – my mini penis that is – compared to Mr. Big John's massive banana sized dick at least.

She began to gently stroke his cock. I could see it in his eyes that he could feel it and it felt amazing. He began to moan as his eyes were squinting in pleasure. He jerked his head back and began to breath heavily. As she kept stroking his cock, he reached down with two fingers and began to massage her tiny little pink pussy. As soon as his fingers made impact with her little pussy, she began to moan.

She began to stroke his massive dick faster and harder as he began to match her speed by fingering her just as fast and just as hard as she was doing him. I could hear the wild slurping sound of his fingers going deeper and deeper into her bodily cave in between her legs. He started with one finger and now he had three fingers going in her. How much more could that little pussy possibly take? I suppose that if it was going to take his big ass dick, then surely he would have to prepare it by shoving as many fingers in it now as he possibly could.

Big John kept fingering away as she was stroking away. Finally, at this point, she dropped to her knees with her hand still on his dick. Then she opened her mouth wide and swallowed his entire, massive, banana sized dick whole and began to suck him off like a champ. Her head was bobbing back and forth as he stood there with pleasure written all over his face. His chest was puffed out as if he was proud

– as he if he was a pussy hunter and was proudly showing off the trophy he caught.

She was taking every inch of his dick and was doing so without hesitation or error. He grabbed her by the hair and was holding on tight as she began to suck him harder and faster. With each suck, he began to thrust her to the point where he was fucking her mouth, treating her like a true whore – which is exactly how my wife loved to be treated.

With her mouth still swallowing his dick, he stepped over to the couch and then sat down and spread his legs wide. She kept sucking away as he sat there taking it. He dropped his head back and began to enjoy and take in the ride, loving every second of pleasure that my wife was giving him. She began to rub his balls smoothly. His eyes closed and it was obvious he really liked this. Then she pulled out, went down and begin to lick his asshole clean. She was licking it all over like it was a pussy and she was a man going down on it, but just the opposite in fact. She was tossing his salad and covering it in her saliva. He was groaning and really getting into it.

He grabbed his fat, banana sized dick and began to jerk it off roughly and quickly as she kept digging into his asshole with her tongue. His head was jerking back as his eyes were sealed shut. He was making all of these crazy faces, which were all a reaction to the intense pleasure he was receiving from her.

My dick was hard and I wanted to snatch it out and jerk it off but refrained. It simply wasn't time yet.

She then opened wide and swallowed his balls, massaging them with her tongue. She was like an animal with her mouth. It is officially safe to say she was putting on a show for Big John – and of course for myself as I was enjoying it almost as much as he was – well, judging by the crazy look on his face, maybe not quite as much as he was enjoying it, but still, I was fucking enjoying this shit. I had the greatest wife ever!

And so she finished up licking his balls and stood up before bending over right in front of me, poking her ass out. Her ass was incredible. It was plump and smooth and that little asshole just opened up like a rose just above her cunt.

She started kissing Big John again as he reached behind her and stuck his finger back inside of her pussy. He began fingering her again as she made out with him. She then returned the favor by reaching down, grabbing his big ass dick and jerking it off. They were finger fucking each other while making out. She was still bent over and I could see everything on her end with great detail. It was an amazing sight to behold. This was by far my favorite wife fucking adventure and they truly hadn't even started fucking yet! They were still in foreplay mode.

As he kept fingering her pussy while she was jerking his big ass dick, he suddenly shoved his thumb into her tight little asshole, giving her the shocker. She let out a quick scream before moaning as he began to finger fuck both her pussy and her tight little ass hole. She was moaning and enjoying it. I could see the moisture around her pussy and asshole region just accumulating as she was getting into it, moaning like a wild girl.

They finally stopped as he stood back up, with his tongue still in her mouth. They kept making out while rubbing and feeling all over each other. Then he turned to me, made a wicked face before looking back to her, putting his arms around her waste and then flipping her upside down and planting his face and tongue right into her pussy as he stood there, holding her in the air. He also shoved his big massive dick into her mouth. They were standing there 69'ing. Literally, 69'ing while standing up. I had never seen any shit like this before. It was insane and unreal. She was hanging upside down, sucking on his cock as he held onto her while he was licking her pussy.

He stepped over toward me and through her spread legs, he looked at me with his eyes right above her ass and still gave me that wicked stare which I loved. I was so hot. In fact, I was probably hotter and hornier than this mother fucker was.

Seriously!

He started spinning her around as her hair just danced in the air.

Then, while still 69'ing, he finally slowed down and laid down onto the couch on his back with her still on top of him in the 69 position. She kept sucking him off while he licked her little pussy out. He was going at it fast and hard now, like a predator devouring its prey. She was trying to match his intensity but failed. The pleasure was getting to her and because of that, she could barely even focus on her task at hand: which was sucking his huge ass dick.

Finally, after some time had passed, he slapped her on both ass cheeks. That was her cue to get up and she did.

"Ready to get that little pussy fucked?" He said to her.

"Ohhhh yeah!" She replied before she looked at me and said, "Are you ready, baby?" With the biggest smile on my face, I said, "You know I am! I have been ready!"

"Let's do this shit!" Big John said as he spun her around on top of him. She bent over as her tits just dangled in his face. He grabbed his big ass dick and began to massage the outer lips of her pussy before shoving it right in. I heard a crazy slurping and/or popping noise as it went in. Before she could even react, he started hammering her like he was fucking superman going faster than a speeding bullet. He was going so fast, I shit you not, it was almost a blur. She was moaning and screaming as even she wasn't expecting this – but it was clear she was loving the hell out of this!

He was so fast, it was unbelievable. I almost wanted to tape it for the world to see. He was a fucking machine – literally! A fucking machine!

I couldn't hold back. I pulled my boxers off and began to jerk my dick and my dick was laughable compared to this man Big John's massive ass banana sized manly cock that was going in and out of my wife like a jackhammer. Hell comparing it to a jackhammer was almost a fucking insult. This was a monster of its own that noting could compare to.

Seeing that big dick with throbbing veins just ram into my wife's wet pussy made me so hot and horny. I was jerking off, watching her body jiggle each time his body clashed into her. Watching sweat pour from his body. Watching him shove his face into her big ass tits. Watching her face just contort and go crazy due to the pleasure he was giving her. It made me so fucking hot and horny…

I kept on jerking my dick to the sight of Big John the stud fucking my wife practically insane. She was screaming in pleasure. Her body was tensing up as tight as possible. Her head was twisting and turning like she was possessed. I swear I'd never been turned on this badly before. I started stroking my dick harder and harder and harder. It was almost as if the harder I stroke it, the harder he fucked her…

Suddenly, from out of nowhere, he stopped on a dime. Then he flipped her around in the reverse cowgirl position. But strangely, he didn't fuck her. He quickly stood up while holding her in the same position. Now he was holding her as her body hovered above the ground as he stood there and began to light her up – while standing and holding her in the reverse cowgirl… Her face was just above mine. She was sporting a horrific look on her face… but it was all due to the intense pleasure she was getting from Big John himself.

Seeing these two in this very position brought me back to the very first time I ever saw my wife get fucked by another man. It was the man who started this great tradition for her and myself.

His name was Henry. We didn't know much about him – at least I didn't anyway. He was slim, but ripped up like a chicken and he had the stamina of a fucking freak of nature. He pounded my wife in every position you could think of. The first time I had ever seen a position so crazy – similar to the position Big John currently had my wife in - was that time with Henry. My wife's first "other man". The man who started this annual tradition for us that we hold near and dear to our hearts.

Yes, he fucked my wife like a rag doll and it all started with this wacky position that Big John had my wife in. It was as if he was paying homage to that, even though he had no clue. But to me and my wife – well, she was getting fucked so hard at the current moment, she had no clue – it was as if he was paying homage.

He started spinning her around in circles while tearing her pussy a new one. I just knew they had to be getting dizzy because hell, I was getting dizzy just watching them. Then, after a few more spins on the big John train, he walked over to the couch and dropped her down onto it and while keeping his dick still inside of her, he began to fuck her from behind – doggie style.

He was ramming that shit hard and as fast as he possibly could. His tight ass – that was sweaty and pouring with sweat at that – was clinching up with every thrust. He had a good looking ass for a dude. Seeing him flinch it each time he rammed his huge ass dick into my wife's tight little pussy got me closer and closer over the edge. Keep in mind, I was still jerking off and close to blowing.

I watched as his balls dangled and flew all over the place as he kept on ramming my wife as hard and as fast as he possibly could. His entire body looked amazing. It was covered in sweat and he was flexing – or should I say "showing off" – with each thrust of his physically impressive body.

I could see my wife just reaching for the top of the couch. She would grip it hard, then release it. Her hands would then fly all over the place before they landed on another part of the couch, gripping it tightly. Then she would repeat the same motions. She did not honestly know what the fuck she was doing and neither did I. She was out of her bloody mind and did not care in the slightest. She did not have a care in the world other than Big John's big ass dick being shoved inside of her and that was it. Anything could have happened and she would not give a single shit at this point. The house could catch on fire and she would ignore it. A guy could just waltz into our apartment, steal everything we own and she wouldn't even bother to chase him – not as long as Big John's big dick was stabbing her little pussy.

He finally pulled out and allowed her to suck on it a moment while he took a break. He laid down on the couch as she crawled down onto his dick and began sucking him off. He just relaxed and closed his eyes as she licked all over his long and hard ass dick. She would lick his dick, followed by his balls and then his ass hole. It was the perfect moment of relaxation for Big John. She then grabbed his dick and began to jerk it while she sucked it and licked all over it. She could literally use two hands to stroke it and still fit a large portion of it in her mouth. It was that fucking big.

Of course, I was watching like Hawkeye and jerking away at my little pencil dick compared to his anaconda of a cock. At one point while she was sucking, she actually turned to me and smiled before focusing back on the task at hand and continuing to suck and jerk his long ass dick.

She was slurping away before he had finally had enough. He straightened her up and grabbed her legs. He then spread them wide and dropped her onto his dick as he still laid there. Then he began to fuck her hard and fast, basically picking up where he left off last. She entered that other state of mind – her pleasure mode I suppose – as her head began bobbling as she drooled and screamed in intense pleasure.

He was rocking her hard as she bounced up and down on that dick. A few minutes passed and he sprung up, face to face with her, and wrapped his arms around her. Then she began to hump him as they sat face to face, holding each other tight. He was licking all over her face and then shoved his tongue into her mouth. She kept on riding him. He then bent down and began to suck her boobs. He would lick and suck on one and then jump over and do the same to the other.

I was ready to cum. Keep in mind I was still jerking my dick. Since they were both sitting up, there was plenty of free space on the couch. I decided to rush over to them to get a better look – up close and personal. I know they wouldn't mind – especially my wife – as they knew the agreement and me being there was part of it.

I bent down, underneath my wife and basically facing his dick that she was hopping up and down on. It was covered in her pussy juice. That smell of his balls combined with her pussy that was beaten out was an aroma that could stimulate anyone. It didn't stink, at least in my opinion. It was a smell that actually served as yet another huge turn on for me.

I kept jerking it as I sat right there face to face with the action. And then, I exploded all over the place. I kept my eyes on the two fuck birds as I came everywhere. And then, I ran back over to my spot and took a seat and continued to watch. What a fucking rush that was! It was incredible. And to them, they acted like I was never there. Hell, I don't even think they truly noticed me to be honest with you.

Big John then lifted her up into the air once again and began to power fuck her while holding her. It was almost like a workout for him in the gym. He had her damn legs hiked above his head as he held her tight and bounced her up and down on his dick in mid air as he stood there holding her.

He stepped down off the couch and then dropped her onto the ground, on her back. He hovered above her and slid his dick back into where it so rightfully belonged: her pussy. He grabbed her legs, hiked them back over his shoulders once again and began to light her pussy up. He was fucking her so hard, you could literally feel the ground shaking. It was almost like a very small earthquake.

After about ten minutes or so, he reached over and grabbed a nearby bottle of lube. As he was still fucking her, he managed to pour half the bottle onto her ass hole.

Then he pulled out, grabbed his dick and shoved it right into her ass. Her eyes lit up like a Christmas tree as he started tearing her asshole a new one.

"That is so fucking tight!" He exclaimed as she just screamed at the top of her lungs. He continued smashing her ass, as he bent her over, angling her ass into the air, dropping his dick missile down into her turd tunnel. He kept going. It was 100% pure pounding!

"Where do you want me to cum? Huh? Where do you want me to cum?" He asked her. But she couldn't respond. She was too mentally fucked up due to the insane fuck he was administering on her body. It was as if she didn't hear him and thus, he elected to improvise instead. He kept on humping away and I could see the climax brewing in both his body and his eyes. His eyes were beaming and locked on to her. They weren't moving nor was he blinking. His body kept tensing up with every thrust. Tighter and tighter and tighter. Sweat began to pour down his body like rain. And then, he snapped that cock out, grabbed it and began to jerk it right above her pussy. It didn't take but a second and then he came all over her pussy region. He was moaning like a man fighting a turd on the toilet. I could only imagine how great this felt for him.

Finally, he stopped and as per our tradition, I walked over and cleaned my wife off with a clean towel. It was my duty as the bitch ass cuckold husband to do so. He soaked her pretty good as cum was everywhere – from her belly button to her gooch – she was covered in his very own semen.

After it was all said and done, my wife could barely stand on her own unassisted. But after she came to, we both thanked him and he happily thanked us as well. She then looked to me and whispered into my ear: "He was by far the best, honey. Is there any way you could go ahead and reserve him for next year?"

Of course, what my baby wants, my baby gets. That is how I feel at least. And so, before Mr. Big John left our humble abode, I pulled him aside and asked him if we could go ahead and book him in advance for next year as well. He simply looked me in the eyes with a big smile on his face and said, "Of course. I had such a great time with your wife, I'm willing to do it next year for free. No charge."

When I told my wife the great news, she was so ecstatic, she could barely contain herself. Next thing you know, she was starting a countdown for next year… counting down the days until Big John returned for the grand sequel to fuck her into submission yet again. Hell, we were both looking forward to it as was he I'm sure…

The Unwilling Cuckold:
My Girlfriend Gets Destroyed By A Body Builder

Let me start things off by telling you a little bit about my current girlfriend and myself. We have been together for a little over a year now and first met at a mutual friend's birthday party.

We hit it off instantly and became very close.

A year later, our relationship had gotten a little rocky. We're not as close as we once were and now, all we seem to do is fight more than we actually get along or talk about anything else. To top it all off, we hadn't had sex in a very, very long time.

I found a nice little beach house which was secluded on a small beach town roughly four hours from where we live. I rented the house online and ended up talking briefly with the guy who owned the home over the phone. He was kind of an ass and spoke with a real deep and cocky voice. After it was all said and done, I managed to secure this beach house for the upcoming weekend for $500 for three nights, which I thought was a steal.

I hadn't talked to my girlfriend in two days but managed to reach out to her and tell her about it. The only reason I wanted to do this was to try and reignite our sputtering relationship so that we could become close to each other once again.

After practically begging her to accept this invitation she finally did, which made me feel a little better.

The following weekend came and I had everything packed, loaded up my car and drove over to her house. I pulled into her driveway and knocked on her door. She opened it without even really looking at me. She walked right by me, carrying her on luggage and loaded her luggage into my car herself. That's how awkward our relationship had gotten, but luckily, I planned on straightening things out during our little weekend getaway to the beach.

So we got in the car and started our long, four hour journey to the beach. It was very awkward to start with as neither one of us really ly said anything to each other. I could tell she didn't want to be bothered as she just sat there and played on her phone for the longest time. Each time I tried to start a conversation, she would shut it down instantly.

I honestly don't know what started our relationship downfall. Throughout the silent drive, I tried to think of where it started going south but there never really was a breaking point to be honest. It's just like over time, we grew apart and now I think the only reason she's still with me is simply because she is afraid to hurt my feelings. I think she realized I was a loser and she no longer wanted to be with me but because she was a nice person, as was I, she simply doesn't want to hurt my feelings. But I am truly hoping that this trip and doing all of this for her will put a smile on her face just as I used to do when we first got together.

After some time, I did manage to get a little bit out of her. She told me about work and all the stress she's been under, which I actually did not know about. She told me about her mother, brother, co-workers, friends, etc. She actually started warming up to me and I liked it. It's as if she was opening up and felt comfortable talking to me. So I just sat back and let her talk away.

I didn't know she had been under so much pressure and she told me she needed something to help relieve her of all the pressure and stress she had been under. Thankfully, this trip was going to be the perfect solution for her stress and worries.

And so we arrived into town and I managed to get the guy who owned the house on the phone. He was supposed to be meeting us at the place to give me the key to the house and so I could also pay him. We were merely a few minutes away and he said he would be running behind but we could wait there at the house, which I was cool with.

And so we pulled up at the location and my jaw dropped. It was drop dead gorgeous and located directly on the beach. Literally, the backyard was nothing but the ocean shore. It was paradise. We decided to get out and walk around and right away, my girlfriend reentered bitch mode — like all that talking we did on the way down here in the car never happened. She was back to being her old self but I didn't care. I knew this trip would hopefully cheer her up and make her want me again. She said she needed something to help her and I knew this house and being on the beach on top of that would be the perfect cure to her stress and worries.

So we walked around the house and peeked through the windows. It was a small, one bedroom house but it didn't matter. It was perfect and just spacious and luxurious enough for the both of us. There was a patio that surrounded the entire house and like I said, the backyard was the beach so no one could complain about this place. I circled the place as my girlfriend stayed behind, looking through a window on the porch.

My phone began to ring as I saw a black BMW pull into the driveway. It was the guy who owned the house. He got out and was bald headed, dressed fairly classy and he was a young, attractive guy. Not as young as me, but in his mid 30s, which I was not expecting.

He immediately noticed my girlfriend when he got out of the car and approached her. I saw her turn around to look at him and she was almost in a state of shock. Needless to say, I didn't understand why. I figured she liked his car or something.

As I approached, I noticed they were engaged in a conversation with one another. I stood there and neither one of them even acknowledged me or said a word to me. It was as if I did not exist in either of their eyes. So I crossed my arms and waited… waited… and waited. Then he looked at me and instead of introducing himself, he said, "Are you ready to see the place?"

I did not know what else to say or do so I just simply nodded my head. He pulled out a key and then proceeded to unlock the door. He motioned for my girlfriend to go in first and then cut in front of me. Then as I walked in, he closed the door behind me. I noticed my girlfriend could not stop looking at him and this was puzzling. I could not figure out why and tried to keep negative thoughts out of my head. Then she told me to go look around the house and so I did. I did not know what else to do or what she was leading on and so I walked into the bedroom to scope out the bed in person. It was nice and actually smelt amazing. All I could imagine was how happy she would be here and how I was going to make her weekend!

I did not know what was going on in there with them but did not pay it any mind either. I was doing as she instructed, which was to check out the house. And so I looked in the bathroom and also the massive walk in closet. It was the perfect getaway house! And I could not wait to spend this weekend with her.

Then, just as I turned around and started to head for the door, all of a sudden, my girlfriend and the home owner came bursting through the door, tangled up in each other's arms and making out. His shirt was already halfway unbuttoned to top it off.

At first, I froze, not knowing what to do. Was this real or was my imagination running wild? It didn't take but a few seconds to pass before I realized this was a reality and my current girlfriend was making out with a guy she just met right in front of me. My jaw dropped and I began to feel anxious. I could do nothing here, hell, I didn't know what to do. All this time she said she needed something to relieve the stress, here she was, about to get it. She found it in the man who was renting a vacation home to me (and one I was paying for – not her) and he was about to give it to her.

Things were heating up as their breathing intensified. They were both feeling all over one another and acting as if I was invisible. I could not take this anymore. I almost had to pinch myself to believe it was all real – and it was. So finally, I stepped toward them and spoke up.

"What the hell is going on?" I asked.

They didn't bother acknowledging me at first. Their minds were strictly focused on each other. But then, without even looking at me, he made the comment, "What does it look like?"

They continued making out as they shoved their tongues in each other's mouths. She finally had his shirt fully unbuttoned as he threw it off himself to reveal a huge, burly and ripped up body. It was a sight to behold and it put my little scrawny, weakling body to shame.

He worked out and it was obvious.

Then, as he continued making out with her, he managed to say to me, "She's working to pay off your rent for the weekend."

I did not even know how to respond to that at first. It took me a second and then I replied, "I am going to pay you in cash, though. Enough of this!"

That's when he said, "Oh no! Your girlfriend and I have already made a deal and we're sealing it as we speak."

I was at a loss and clearly taken aback by this. Just when I tried to say something else, that's when she finally stopped, broke away and looked at me with fire in her eyes and said, "Would you shut the fuck up?"

And again, I froze, not knowing what the hell to say or do. Then, he just had to chime in as well by saying, "Listen to this sexy ass lady because if you don't, I'll shut you the fuck up."

And so I had no choice but to sit there in silent and watch as my girlfriend of one year was about to fuck some guy who was supposed to rent a beach house out to me for the weekend – a guy she had just fucking met to top it all off and that makes it even worse.

She began to rub his burly body as he managed to snatch her shirt off. Her tits just dangled as she kept feeling all over his shirtless and buff chest. Then, he ripped her bra off with ease, grabbed both of her tits with his hands and began to lick them all over.

I could tell she was wanting him so badly it was causing her so much stress. Her breathing was intensifying as he was know sucking on her tits – and he was sucking them hard. He was squeezing them just as hard as he was sucking.

Then, he broke away and pulled his pants off. As he stood there in his boxers, I could see a massive dick poking out. I didn't even want to imagine the rest as I knew I was about to see it up close and personal first hand.

She then gently jerked his boxers down as a big, massive, 7 and a half inch throbbing cock slapped her in the face. Without even taking a breath, she grabbed that cock and swallowed it whole and began to suck on it like she was an award winning porn star.

I never saw her suck my dick the way she was doing his nor did I ever see her crave my dick the way she was craving his. This was complete and utter humiliation.

She kept sucking his dick before he finally shoved her away, grabbed her tits and then shoved his dick in between her perky little perfect titties. He began to roughly titty fuck her back and forth back and forth back and forth with great speed.

This was intense! As he was doing so, she titled her head down, opened up her mouth and caught the head of his dick with each thrust.

He was moaning and groaning as this had to have felt amazing to him. This was also something I never did with her and something I only wish I had.

Every thrust seemed to get harder and faster. I could not turn away, even knowing the horrifying even this was leading to: full blown vaginal penetration.

After he finished up titty fucking her, he stood her up and yanked off her pants. She was breathing profusely, wanting his cock so badly.

She stood there in her blue little thong and grabbed his cock, jerking it as she waited for him to do whatever he planned on doing next.

Then he squatted down and began to rub her pussy as he licked all over her torso. She started taking long, deep breaths as her sexual anxiety was intensifying.

Then, he pulled her blue little thong off and shoved his tongue right into her pussy and began licking it.

She squealed like a little girl as this felt great to her. It had been a long time since her pussy was touched and I know that to her, this was well worth the wait.

He then wrapped his arms around her, picked her up, spun her upside down in a standing 69 position and began to eat her pussy out while she sucked his dick. I had never seen this bizarre position before and I know she hadn't either. With his huge dick in her mouth, she was moaning while making slurping sounds.

He would spin and turn, at one point even facing me with those dark eyes staring a hole through me as he ate out the pussy I once fucked while my soon to be ex girlfriend had his dick in her mouth.

Then he dropped her on to the bed and climbed on top, still in the 69 position. Her head was hanging off the bed as he spread his legs wide and began to hump her mouth with his dick still inside of it.

I could see his muscular ass cheeks spread wide open. I could see his dark asshole opened up. I could see his balls slapping my girlfriend in the nose each time he dropped down on her.

This was insane!

And after a few more minutes, he stood up, with his dick still inside of her, and fucked her mouth while standing. He only did this for a minute before jumping onto the bed. She jumped up as well, climbed on top of him, spread her legs wide open and squatted down, consuming his entire dick with her wide open vagina.

She let out a serious moan just before he began to light her up. He started pumping that pussy with his dick fast, almost at light speed. The smacking sound of their two bodies colliding together was deafening. She was moaning and screaming in intense pleasure. This was the hardest and fastest fucking I had ever seen in my life. No porn star could top this dude and it was obvious – not just by his amazing body – he worked out based on how hard he was fucking her. I couldn't do half that.

He kept on pumping before he spun her around with haste and started fucking her at the same speed – hard and fast – in the reverse cowgirl position. I could see her face as her eyes were rolled up into the back of her head. Her mouth was wide open and her tongue was hanging out. This dude was literally fucking her senseless.

His long, hard and massive dick was splitting her tight little wet pussy wide open. Seeing it go in and out in and out in and out at that speed was incredible. I still couldn't believe this was happening right in front of me.

In one quick motion, he pushed her forward on her hands and knees, propped himself up – all without taking his dick out of her - and began to fuck her doggie style. All I could hear was the sound of her moaning loudly and the crashing sound of their two bodies colliding with one another.

At this point, the initial shock had worn off and all I could do was sit and watch while taking mental notes on how to properly please my next girlfriend. Of course, I would have to start by working out if I wanted to reach his stamina and speed.

I sat there and observed as he continued pounding out my girlfriend from behind. As long as this had been doing on, it still hadn't gotten old.

By this point, the room began to reek of sweat and sex. That was all my nose could smell.

Then, he pulled out, spun her around and shoved his cock – that was covered in her pussy juice – into her mouth as he began drilling her mouth once again. He was drilling her face with no remorse. He looked at me and smirked before pulling out and standing her up, planting her face into the wall.

They both stood on the bed as he entered her pussy again from behind. He began to fuck her fast and hard from behind as the sound of her being fucked against the wall rattled the walls. Her hands were pressed firmly against the wall. The side of her face was planted into the wall as her eyes were closed, mouth was wide open and drool was starting to drip from her mouth.

Meanwhile, he was just slamming his dick into her as hard as he could. Her body was crashing against the head rest, jamming it into the wall.

Then he pulled out, grabbed her and they both fell into the bed, tangled in each other's arms. Then, with her on top, he slammed his dick back into her and began fucking her once again.

While doing so this time, he started sucking on her tits as she screamed in pleasure.

Again, all I could hear was the sound of him groaning which was almost being drowned out by the sound of her screaming in pleasure and the deafening sound of his body slamming into her body.

I knew she had to be numb but judging by her screams, she wasn't. She was full blown into this!

This was the best action she had ever received and the best fuck she had ever gotten. It totally erased any terrible memory of all the mediocre and laughably bad fucks that I gave her.

The fucking continued as by now, he was flipping her onto her back and threw her legs into the air. He entered her once again and began driving her while on top. She kept moaning while he groaned. I could hear his groans getting louder as he was close to climaxing.

He kept pumping, and it seemingly got harder and faster as every second passed.

Then, he yanked that fat and long, soaking wet dick out and jumped up to her face, shoving it into her mouth. He began fucking her face once again as his groans grew louder and then… he slowed down as he began to blow loads of cum all into her mouth. She laid there and took it like a champ, swallowing every bit of it.

Then he pulled out, stood up and placed his clothes back on as she just laid on the bed, motionless and breathing hard and fast, trying to get over the hardest and best fuck she had ever received in her entire life.

As he finished dressing himself, he tossed me the key and smiled with a wicked look on his face and said, "Your debt is paid, buddy. Stay here as long as you guys want."

Then, just like that, he walked out and left, getting what he wanted.

Meanwhile, my girlfriend was still laying on her back, not saying a word and still trying to catch her breath while getting over the high of the greatest fuck she had ever received.

I stood up and walked over to the bed and noticed she was covered head to toe in sweat. She was soaking wet. I also noticed there were wet spots all over the bed from where they were sweating.

I did not know what to say or do. All I could do is look and think about how it was time to turn my life around. I needed to get in shape because I now knew how to properly fuck and please a woman – and it was all thanks to my now ex-girlfriend and this handsome homeowner with a massive cock.

I tossed the key on the bed beside her and walked out the door.

Watching My Enemy With My Wife: Becoming A Pathetic Cuckold

I had just reached the five minute mark at work. It was a very long and shitty day. My coworkers also happened to be in a foul mood along with all the entitled and arrogant clients I have to deal with. To top it all off, my wife and I had been fighting a lot lately after she discovered I had an account on an adult fuck site. Granted I had never actually met or been with anyone from the site, I set it up weeks ago when my wife and I's relationship started to truly spiral down hill.

I just couldn't take it anymore. We were once best friends and now we're best of enemies. I don't know why I did it. I wasn't going on there actually searching for pussy, I was merely doing it just to see what was out there. No harm done and I had no intentions of actually getting with another woman. But I couldn't tell her that.

There was no reasoning with her. She had absolutely lost her mind and officially hated me now.

But of all the fights we had here of late, last night was the worst. It almost got physical. I saw something in her eyes I never thought I'd see. I could tell she truly hated me and although I was nowhere near that level, it was almost scary. She screamed bloody murder at me, telling me how much she hated me and that she would get the last laugh.

I was sitting there dreading having to go home. As shitty as work was that day, it still couldn't top whatever was going to happen in that sinister house of mine. I could only imagine what lied ahead.

And thus, that time had finally come. It was time for that quick ride home to face the sheer terror that awaited me. I took my dear sweet time clocking out and heading for the parking lot. I was clearly in no rush, despite finishing up one of the worst work days in my work existence. I got in my car and left.

For the first time ever, I was happy to be sitting in rush hour traffic. I did not mind it in the slightest. Usually, rush hour is the worst part of my day but today, it wasn't so bad after all.

All day even up until this point, I hadn't gotten a single call or text from my wife. I guess last night's huge fight was officially the proverbial straw that broke the camel's humps. I knew when I stepped foot through my front door, it would be bad. Something very bad was going to happen. It was going to be the bloody horrific sequel to the shit show that was last night.

After an hour of happily sitting in rush hour traffic, I finally pulled into my modest little one story suburban home. I parked. I turned the car off. Then I sat there. Sat there collecting my courage. Sat there pondering on life. Sat there making sure my balls were still in place. I knew I was about to step in to a battle zone, but what kind of battle was anyone's guess. But it was time. It was time for me to both face my fears and also face the great unknown.

So I stepped out of my car and walked up to my front door. I stood there a moment, gathering my courage. I took a deep breath. Then – as tentative as I could possibly be – I reached for the door knob and opened the door. To my surprise, my wife wasn't standing there flipping me off and calling me names. To my surprise, she was screaming at the top of her lungs from another room. To my surprise, she didn't come storming in from another room once she heard me enter the house. To my surprise, it was quiet and I was alone. This isn't so bad!

So I walked in and did what I do everyday I get home: head straight for my bedroom and unwind.

As I said, this wasn't so bad and a perfect way to end a bad day if you ask me.

So I walked up to my bedroom door and opened, not expecting what I was about to encounter. As soon as I opened the door and stepped in, the door slammed behind me, scaring the living shit out of me. I turned to see my wife and my biggest enemy, Dan Terry, standing there against the door.

I hated Dan. He was a guy who bullied me in high school and

even into our early adult years, he rivaled everything I did. He was physically superior to me, so I could not kick his ass. But I still hated him with every fiber of my being. I swear everything he did, he did to spite me. So what the fuck was he doing in this house?

"What the fuck is going on?" I asked my wife.

"Oh, you know what the fuck is about to go on, fuck boy!" She screamed. That is when Dan stepped forward and grabbed me by the neck and said, "Just when you thought it couldn't get any worse with me, now I'm gonna make you watch me fuck your precious wife."

What the fuck! My wife knew I hated Dan. She absolutely knew it. The guy probably wouldn't even fuck her if he knew she wasn't with me. He was waaaaaay out of her league. Little does this bitch know, he doesn't even give a damn about her. He is only doing it to spite me once again. But I'm sure she doesn't care because she's about to do this to spite me as well.

So I had no choice but to watch this piece of shit fuck my soon to be ex wife. Before anything else happened, he patted me on the back and said, "Just stand right here and be a good little bitch... and I know you're great at being a little bitch."

I wanted to hit this fucker so bad but refrained. I kept my composure best I could because I knew I was no match for this piece of shit dude and I knew he could kick my ass – but I still despised him more than I despise terrorists.

So he walked up to my wife, grabbed her firmly as they both stared each other in the eyes like two young love birds. Then he snatched her close, wrapped his arms around her as tight as he could, stuck his tongue out and then shoved it right into her mouth as they began making out.

She kept peaking over at me while they were making out and I could tell by that teasing look in her eyes she was taunting me and enjoying every second of it. Not just over the fact that she was about to fuck my sworn enemy, but over the fact that she was about to fuck him right before my very eyes.

He then pulled his tongue out and began to lick her face. He was going crazy, licking her all over like a damn untamed dog. He then shoved his tongue into her ear as her eyes closed. At this point, it was no longer a taunting session for her as she was feeling the heat. She was growing horny.

Out the billions of stupid things that have happened to me in my life, this was by far the stupidest. This was by far the most humiliating. It's not just the fact that my wife is cheating on me just as it's not just the fact that she is doing it right before my very eyes… it's the fact that she is fucking the one person in this bloody universe who I hate the most – and she's doing it right in front of me and forcing me to watch. I never hated my wife but now, I hate her probably more than I hate this jackass.

He was rubbing and feeling all over her and she was doing the same. Her hands were sliding up his shirt. Then in one rather swift motion, he snatched her shoulder straps from her dress off and her dress fell to the ground revealing she had no panties or underwear on. His eyes lit up like a freaking Christmas tree.

"Oh yeah, that is what I like to see," he said while gazing at her tits. Then he looked over at me with a sinister smirk and said, "watch this, bitch."

He opened his mouth wide and then bent over, taking in as much of her right titty as he could. He started sucking and licking all over it. She began to moan as he continued to suck away like it was a feast. He then reached up and started grabbing all over her free titty. He was rubbing and massaging it while sucking the other.

Then he started going back and forth, sucking and licking on each titty, taking turns with each of them. He then stopped and backed away before rubbing all over them.

"Yes, these are very nice fucking titties. My dick wants to meet them." He said. Then he turned to me and said, "I'm going to introduce my dick to your wife's titties. How do you like that shit?" He smiled sinisterly once again and then began to take off his clothes. Piece by piece: his shirt, his pants, his shoes, his socks and then his underwear.

His body was surprisingly disgusting. He was out of shape with man boobs, a beer belly and was covered in hair. His dick was a complete black bush of hair. But his dick was actually in great shape and was shockingly big. It was long, fat and rock fucking hard.

My wife hated hairy dudes but she didn't seem to mind him in the slightest. Her eyes just sparkled when she saw his dick. Without saying a word and without hesitation, she dropped to her knees and took that big hairy dick right in her little mouth. She began to suck that thing like dick sucking was going out of style. She was showing out, sucking it like a porn star because she knew and I knew as well that she never sucked my dick like that. Hell, most of the time she hated sucking dick. She found it to be gross and hated doing it. But here, she had zero problems sucking off this guy's fat hairy cock.

He began to moan and smile. He looked up to the ceiling and then over at me and said, "You like that? Huh? You like seeing that dirty little whore you're married to suck on my fat ass cock? Yeah, you like that shit don't you? You fucking love it! Guess what? I know I do. I fucking love that shit. Yes! I fucking love having your wife's lips swallowing my fat ass dick whole! Ohhh yeah!" Then he focused back on her as she continued to suck his hard ass dick like a champion.

It was a purely disgusting sight that made me want to gag. But I had no choice but to sit there and watch as this man violated my bitch of a wife whom I officially hated now. In fact, hate isn't the appropriate word. There are absolutely no words in the English dictionary to describe my true negative feelings I had for her now. She crossed the line big time by even thinking about fucking this piece of shit for a man. I could not stand him and now because of this, I could not stand her ass even more.

They kept going at it like it was nothing. She was sucking and tugging on his dick like a pro while he stood there and moaned and groaned, enjoying every second of her little lips on his dick. He reached down and began massaging her tits again as she continued to suck him off.

Then he pulled out and I saw a string of spit connecting from the tip of his dick to her mouth. It eventually broke as he stood her up, stuck his nasty ass tongue out and then shoved it into her mouth. As they made out again, she began to jerk his dick with her hand as he started rubbing and massaging all over her boobs once again.

After a few minutes of a continuous nonstop make out session passed, he broke away and forced her over to the bed. She laid down on her back and spread her legs wide open. He then turned around to me with that shit eating sinister smile on his face and said, "You want to see my tongue in your wife's pussy? Watch… watch as I lick her like an ice cream cone."

He then turned around to her and bent over, sticking his tongue out and shoving it into her pussy. He began licking her out all over the place. She gripped the bed and begin to loudly moan. I could tell when her moans were fake and real and these moans were fucking real. She meant it and it pissed me off even more. It was legit and I hated this shit.

I looked down to see him bent over and all I saw was a nasty black hairy asshole staring me down. It was grotesque and disgusting. I could not believe she was allowing this nasty man with an even nastier body do this to her. It was head scratching to say the least. He began to bounce up and down as he was licking her out harder and harder. About five more minutes or so passed and then he got up. Even though he broke away from her, she was still moaning in crazed pleasure as she laid there like a statue with her eyes focused on the ceiling.

"Watch what I am about to do to your wife, asshole," he said to me. And all I could do was sit and watch, humiliated, shamed and pissed off beyond belief.

He crawled onto the bed and laid down on his back. She got up and crawled on top of him. He spun her around, placing her pussy right in his face as she dropped down onto his cock as they began 69'ing each other. All I could hear were the disgusting sounds of slurping, sucking, licking, moaning and groaning.

They 69'd for quite some time until they finally grew bored with it. Then she stood up and spun around as his rock hard fat and hairy dick just pointed directly up to the ceiling. She spread her legs wide and looked over at me and winked with a big smile on her face. He then looked to me with that familiar shit eating sinister grin and said, "say goodbye to your wife's innocence, bitch. She is my property now! All. Fucking. Mine!"

With her legs spread wide, she dropped down onto his cock and began to ride it up and down up and down up and down. She was moaning loudly. It was so loud, it gave me an ear ache and a head-ache. She wasn't faking it either and that made matters even worse.

He started groaning and moaning with his eyes closed. He was grunting as well, just enjoying the feeling of her nice little warm pussy – a feeling I used to enjoy as well but not anymore!

He reached up and started grabbing her titties. He was squeezing them hard and all over. It was almost as if he was holding on to them for dear life because she was riding his dick as hard as she possibly could. She bent down and grabbed his shoulders, gripping them tight as her ass just kept going up and down up and down up and down.

They were going at it like animals and it was a sight to behold.

As she continued to squeal and moan, he cried as loud as he could, "Oh, yes! That is great pussy! That is great fucking pussy! Yes it is! Oh… Oh… Ohhhhhh fuck yes!" Then with his eyes closed, enjoying the pleasure, he asked her, "Is this the best dick you've ever had? Huh? Is this the best fucking dick you've ever had? Huh, bitch?"

To the best of her ability, she responded incoherently in be-tween her moans, "Yeah!"

Then he continued by asking, "Who is the real fucking man in the room? Huh? Tell us all who the fuck the real man in the room is!"

And again, she responded to the best of her ability incoherently in between the moans, "You are, daddy! You fucking are!"

And he still continued, "That is fucking right! Take that fucking dick like the champion whore that you are! Take that dick like a champ! Take it like it's the best dick you've ever had!"

The more he said that shit, the harder and harder she drove her pussy into his cock! SMACK! CLAP! SMACK! CLAP! SMACK! CLAP! SMACK! CLAP! SMACK! CLAP! SMACK! CLAP! SMACK! CLAP! SMACK! CLAP! SMACK! CLAP! SMACK! CLAP! SMACK! CLAP!

SMACK! CLAP – along with the deafening sounds of loud moans, grunts, groans and squeals is all I heard resound throughout the room. This was pure fucking torture.

Then, he bent her over, planting her tits right into his piece of shit face. He opened his mouth wide and began to suck on them as he used both hands to spread her ass cheeks wide, gripping both cheeks in the process. With his fat and hard dick still in her pussy, he began to fuck her – and he began to fuck her fast and hard. Almost at lightening speed. He was drilling her with intensity as he had a firm grip on her ass. She was screaming at this point. Screaming like I've never heard her little ass scream before. It was deep, loud and passionate. Her hunger for his cock was being fulfilled right before my two very own eyes.

"Yes, scream, bitch! Fucking scream! Scream for that dick, bitch! Scream!" He said to her as he continued to drive her little pussy home.

He started going faster and faster while fucking her harder and harder. The sound of his body clashing into hers combined with his massive hairy dick smashing her little pussy along with the intense screams, moans, groans and grunts almost sounded like a rap beat. It was a sound no one could recreate or even possibly imagine.

He kept going and going, harder and faster with every hard thrust as her screams grew louder and more intense. As bad as it was and as much torture on me as it was, I simply could not take my eyes off of it. His groans and grunts were getting louder and more intense as well. I honestly could not tell if he was sincere and legit or if he was just doing this to taunt and tease me. Either way, nothing he could further do would make matters even worse than they already were.

He eventually grew tired of this position and then flipped her over onto her back as he spun around on top of her. Before he put it in, he looked back over at me and gave me that same old shit eating sinister grin. Then he calmly said, "You like seeing me fuck your wife? Huh? You like that you piece of shit? Well it ain't over yet. The fun is just getting started, mother fucker."

"Fuck you, bitch!" is of course what I wanted to say in response but I did not bother to say anything. I just sat there like a knot on a log. Like a bitch. I really wanted to tear into this piece of shit mother fucker bad but there was nothing I could do - nothing I could do but sit and watch. But believe me, if I could beat this asshole's ass, I would.

He then looked to my wife who was googly eyed at this point and said, "You ready? Ready for me to keep fucking that tight little pussy?"

Best she could, she incoherently responded, "Uh huh… yeah… uh huh! I want that dick!"

"You want that dick?" He said. "Yeah? You want that fucking dick."

She nodded and once again incoherently uttered, "Yes! Give me that dick! Give it to me! Give it to me right now!"

He looked back at me and said with that same shitty grin, "You hear that, bitch boy? She's demanding me to give her my dick! I'm not gonna deny her demands!" Then he turned to her and said, "Here you go, whore!"

Then he grabbed that long ass dick and stuck it right into her pussy. As soon as it entered, she squealed. Her head snapped back as she gripped the sheets and begin to scream. He began to slam both his dick and body into her as her body shook and the bed slammed into the wall, back and forth like a wave. The head board was SLAMMING into the wall and it was doing it hard. A picture hanging on the wall of my wife and myself fell to the ground due to the hard knocks from the head board. As soon as it hit the ground, it shattered. There was a spider web of cracked glass in between us. It was so symbolic which was perfect for the bullshit that had been happening to us – especially this very moment.

He grabbed her legs and hiked them high into the air above his shoulders in the guillotine position. He wrapped his arms around her legs and gripped them as tight as he could. Then he began going 90 to nothing, fucking the living hell out of her. The bed was rocking like an earthquake – as were their two bodies.

He was covered from head to toe in sweat. It was disgusting as the hair covering his body was all clumped together and moist. It was a revolting sight.

His mouth was open as he was trying to catch his breath from fucking her so hard. But he wouldn't stop. He kept going and going.

She finally let out a loud, "Fuuuuuuuuuuuuck!" as he continued to drive her little pussy home. Then he grunted really loudly before pulling out and flipping her over onto her stomach. She was half worn out and mentally and physically exhausted.

Sweat was pouring from his body so profusely, it was dripping from his head like rain. He was covered in it! He once again looked over at me with that familiar shit eating grin that I was so sick of seeing and said, "Your wife wants it in the ass. Yes, she wants it in her fucking ass! She wants my dick in her ass… yes she does!"

He then formed a big wad of spit in his mouth as he spread her ass cheeks wide open to reveal her tight little untouched asshole. My wife was actually an ass virgin and never would allow me to fiddle around down there nor would she allow any other man to do so. So needless to say, this was a little surprising, although at this point, as crazy as this day and moment was, nothing should surprise me. But this did. That is how crazy the idea of it was. She was strictly against ass fucking. But not anymore of course.

He spit out a big wad of white spit, nailing her right in her little asshole, lubing it up. Then he grabbed his long ass dick and hovered the tip of it right in front of her asshole. He then slowly shoved it in.

His face registered pure pleasure as it was evident this felt amazing to him. Then, like before he started raring back and drilling her little asshole, wearing it out for the first time ever. Not only is this piece of shit fucking my wife right before my very own eyes, here he is taking her ass virginity right before my very own eyes. Just when I thought it could not possibly get anymore humiliating, it did.

She started screaming again. But this was a different scream. It was deep and from the gut. He kept pounding her in the ass as she reached down and begin to finger her little pussy. This was a new adventure for her and she was loving it – every single inch and second of it. His long, fat ass and hairy dick was stretching out my wife's virgin asshole. He was fucking it with no remorse. He was letting loose and going to town in her once untouched ass.

She planted her face into the pillows as he grabbed her by the back of the head, continuing to drill her asshole into oblivion. She was taking deep breaths with each scream. The pleasure she was feeling by having her ass hole stretched out by a monster dick plus being fingered professionally by this man's manly fingers was unmatched. It was a sensation she had never felt before. Ever.

He continued on like it was nothing and her little virgin asshole was taking it like a true champ – like a freaking porn star. At this point, there was nothing that my wife could not handle. He was pounding her out with all his strength and might.

About ten minutes of pure, untamed ass pounding passed before he finally started to slow up. Was he giving up? Was he ready to call it quits? If only I were so freaking lucky... but no, he turned to me again with that tiresome but very familiar shit eating grin on his punchable face and stared me in the eyes. He then said to me, "You think she's done? Nah. She wants more. I'm gonna make your wife suck both her own ass hole and pussy off of my fat ass cock. And she is gonna love it. And you are gonna love seeing the shit. You ready? Huh? Are you fucking ready?"

Of course I was ready. I had seen so much stupid shit that at this point, I was practically and just about immune to any thing he did to her. I was at peace with everything that had gone down and at this point, I was ready for both of them to hurry up and finish so I could go on about my day. I had had enough.

The room absolutely reeked of ass, pussy, sweat and mildew. So in other words, it reeked of hardcore sex that was still in session.

He turned to my wife who at this point was damn near borderline catatonic. She literally had been fucked senseless by this man whom I call my worst enemy. He grabbed her face and said, "Come on, honey. Suck all of your juices off of my long ass dick. Do it. Show your husband how much you wanna taste your own juices. Show him how much you wanna suck my fucking hard ass dick that just fucked you a new one. Do it… NOW!"

And she leaned up like it was nothing as he laid back against the headboard. She crawled down onto his soaking wet dick that had both her pussy and anal juice on it and opened her mouth wide. Then she swallowed every inch of his humongous cock and began to do exactly as he instructed her by sucking her juices off of him. His eyes shut tight as his face cringed in pleasure. He began to moan just before looking over at me and saying, "You see that, mother fucker? You see it? Huh? This bitch is sucking her own shit that came from the inside of her body right off of my dick. Yes! She is sucking that bad mother fucker clean!" He then looked down at her – best he could – and continued, "Yes, baby! Suck that fucking dick! Suck it good! That's right! Polish my dick! I want that mother fucker spotless for the next time I fuck the hell out of you with it."

So there was going to be a next time? Good for them. All I could do was sit back and hope I would not have to sit and watch. I couldn't stomach another fuck session between these two idiots. I had had enough and was long past reaching my boiling point. And so I continued to watch – I watched as my soon to be ex wife sucked his dick clean. He was moaning and groaning as she was sucking him a new one. I couldn't understand why she never wanted to suck my dick like that. Here she was – a woman who hated sucking dick and thought it was gross – was now sucking his dick AFTER he fucked her in both holes. His dick was covered in her fluids but that wasn't stopping her. Not anymore. This was a brand new woman and she was the perfect whore for him. Hell they were perfect for each other!

The build up was coming. His body was flexing and tensing up. The veins in his neck were starting to pop. He was grabbing her hair and grabbing it as tight as he could. He began to hump her mouth as she continued to suck on it. He was close to finally cumming… and believe me when I say I was ready. I was ready to get this shit over with and leave. Start a new life – without my wife.

His groaning grew louder and louder and louder. "Yes! That's it! Keep going, bitch! Keep it fucking going! Oh yeah!" He said to her as his voice grew louder and louder.

And then, he let out one loud groan before snatching her head back, standing up and jerking his dick right before her face. His rock hard dick then exploded as he unleashed seemingly an endless pound of cum all over her once attractive face. After he finished, he fell back onto the bed as she fell down beside him – face completely covered in cum. Then, he flipped me a bird and said in a commanding tone, "Get the hell out of here… unless you want to see round two."

Without hesitation, I bolted for the door. I got in my car, doing my best to erase the horrific visions from my memory that I just saw. I pulled out of my driveway and left to start a new life. Where the road goes from here, who knows? All I know is I'm no longer with her and I'm happy. I suppose at the end of the day, it was totally worth it because now I've learned from my mistakes and I know that repeating them is something I will NEVER do!

The Secret Sex Room:
Unaware I Wanted To Be A Cuckold

My girlfriend and I had had been together for almost eight months. Our relationship was nothing overly spectacular or out of the ordinary. It was merely a stereotypical relationship for two middle classed people in their early 30s. But of course, that was soon to change and our worlds were both about to expand in ways we never saw coming…

Our sex life was average at best. Nothing to brag or write home about. We'd usually start by skipping right past oral 9 times out of ten, swap positions three times and boom, we're done twenty minutes later. That was our sex life in a nutshell.

So eight months into our relationship, we were becoming more open to one another. We were both in the process of "coming out of our shells" so to speak and at this point, there was nothing we were really truthfully holding back from the other. It was all open, honest clarity and transparency.

She invited me over for dinner at her place one evening, like she had done hundreds of times before. She was a great cook and really enjoyed cooking for me. This was simply another ordinary night. Nothing spectacular. Just dinner for two prepared by her at her place. That was it! Before I dive any further into this story, I want to note that in the eight months we had been seeing each other, I had been to her apartment thousands of times (literally, it was a lot – far too many times to count in fact). The very first time I visited her place, she wasted no time giving me a grand tour. It was a simply two bed-room, two bath apartment. Nothing flashy. But as she gave me the tour the very first time I went to her place, she left off showing me the other bedroom. I even inquired about it and all she said was, "you'll find out later on down the road." Of course, at that time, I took it as a no biggie. In fact, all I could think about was the "later on down the road" part. That told me a lot about her already and it told me that she liked me and obviously wanted to stay with me, as long as I did not bother to fuck things up of course, which at this point, I hadn't done so yet.

But, I would find out later on down the road and so I wasn't worried about it and didn't let my curiosity get the better of me. I just let it go away, knowing I would find out at some point in the future or "later on down the road" as she so eloquently put it.

So in the middle of a very nice dinner, as we were sitting across from one another, again keep in mind, this was merely another casual routine night, she looked me in the eye (I was sitting across the table from her) and she simply said, "I want to show you the room."

At first, believe it or not, I didn't understand what she was talking about. It took a moment before I finally realized that she meant the actual room that was off limits to me. That is how little thought I actually put into this mystery room of hers.

So I nodded my head and replied, "Great! When are you gonna show it to me?" "After you finish your meal!" She said.

Of course, a million thoughts began to rush through my mind like a wild flood. What was in there? Was she hiding bodies? No! It couldn't be bodies because there's no foul smell of rotting, decaying bodies lingering throughout her apartment. Was she a drug dealer? Was this room her drug lab? What the hell was in there? Was she a photographer? Was this her dark room where she developed the photos? Does she stalk people and snap photos of them? Is she paparazzi? Is she a private investigator? What the hell? Seriously! What the hell was in this room?

After I allowed my thoughts to calm, I gently asked, "Should I put on a hazmat suit? I mean, seriously, is it safe?"

And she smiled, ear to ear and said, "Of course it's safe. You have nothing to worry about. Let's just say, it's going to be entertaining - for the both of us."

Entertaining? For the both of us? What the hell could she have possibly meant by that? Surely it wasn't a man cave or a game room. So what did she mean by "entertaining – for the both of us"?

I didn't nag her anymore about it. Instead, I hurriedly finished my meal so that I could find out. And I finished rather quickly to say the least. She took my plate, cleaned it, taking her dear sweet time as I stood up and paced around the living room, waiting for her to finish and impatiently waiting for her to show me this "entertaining room" that would be "entertaining - for the both of us."

Finally, she finished up and made her way to the living room. She held her finger up and motioned for me to follow her to which I did. I followed her over to the door where she stopped, turned around and looked me in the eye, almost pleadingly.

Then she said, "Listen, we have been together for a long time. You know me very well now – well enough to know that I'm not insane or crazy."

Okay? I simply nodded my head in agreement.

And then, she continued on by saying, "This may be a surprise to you, but I don't want it to scare you off. It's simply me. It's simply who I am. It's simply what I like. And it's simply what I'd like for you to do as well – with me."

I was still a tad bit confused. Then, she said, "Please, understand when I open this door, you're going to enter into a completely different world."

"Just open it," I said rather impatiently. At this point, my patience wasn't growing thin, it had already grown thin. I was out of guesses, using them all up at the table. I was just ready to see what lied beyond this door. I was ready to see what she was hiding. I was ready to see what the big mystery was. Why was she keeping this from me until "later on down the road?" Well time was officially up and it was time to find out.

And so, she slowly opened the door and stepped in. I followed behind her and stopped as I entered a pitch black room. The room itself didn't reek of dead bodies.

It didn't smell like a dark room would smell. In fact, it was normal. It smelled like the rest of her apartment – which was a combination of candles and air fresheners scattered throughout every single room in her apartment.

And then, she flipped on the lights. The first thing I saw was her face. She stood there in anticipation – almost worried. Not knowing how I would react. Not knowing how I would take this. Not knowing how I would feel about this. She was even more uncertain and on edge than I was. And then, I looked away and what I saw was even more bizarre and even more stunning than I could have possibly imagined…

Every single wall was lined up shelves. They were covered in shelves. And sitting on those shelves was a vast array of dildos and a variety of sex toys I never even knew existed. On the ground, there were sex pads, a sex couch, containers filled with lingerie, whips, more toys, etc. and the strange part was, everything was clean.

Everything was 100% spotless. There was a spec of dirt or dust on anything. It was as if I stepped into a clean room. So the door obviously hasn't stayed locked and she obviously has been in here cleaning. In fact, judging by how clean the room and each of the objects were, it appeared as if she cleaned every single thing a few times each day. Strangely enough, that is how clean and spotless this room and everything inside of it was.

After the awe wore off, I turned my attention back to her and she was still wearing that look of uncertainty – the same look I was previously wearing. Then she raised her eyebrows and as innocently as she possibly could be, she asked, "What do you think? I know it may be overwhelming but it's not as bad as it might seem."

Of course, I didn't know what to think. I mean, don't get me wrong, I thought it was awesome, but on the other hand, what kind of freak was this chick? This was clearly a surprise and a dark and perverted side of her that I never knew existed. And so, all I could say in response was, "I think it's awesome. A bit scary, but awesome. Baby, I had no idea!"

"I know, and I know it's a lot to take in which is why I didn't want to just throw this on you at first. Listen, I love sex. I'm addicted to it. I also love you and I knew I couldn't keep this from you. I just had to fill you in," she said to me.

"I thank you for doing it. So... what do we do? I'm a bit clueless at this point!" I said in response.

Then she walked up to me as seductively as she possibly could. She wrapped her arms around me and leaned into my ear and whispered, "I know what we can do and I'm going to do it to you." Then she pulled back and gave me a commanding look and said, "Don't be intimidated. Just enjoy what's coming to you."

Then all of a sudden, a side of her personality I've never seen before jumped out. She ran and jumped into my arms, spreading her legs around my waste. She started making out with me and pushed me over toward the corner of the room. I kept going further and further back as she was forcing me to do so. I knew I was going to crash into the wall soon but she was so strong and powerful, I couldn't control it. Like I said, I've never seen this side of her before so I was still a bit shocked as well.

I kept going back, further and further and further until.... I tripped and fell into something hanging from the ceiling – a sex swing! I couldn't believe I didn't even notice this thing. I was so distracted and factor in how shocked I was, this was practically invisible to me. So this is why she was forcing me over here. She started ripping off my clothes as she forcefully rocked the swing back and forth. This was actually quite fun and I was enjoying myself.

Keep in mind, our sex was basically routine. I'll have to remind you that we always skipped foreplay 9 times out of ten and went straight for good old fashioned dick to vagina sex. We would swap positions three times and then be done roughly twenty minutes later. It was nothing exciting, just casual and routine. So this, especially how freaky she was acting, was completely new for me.

By now, she had ripped all of my clothes off and I was laying there with a boner. My dick was simply average sized. Nothing more or nothing less. She liked it though so that's all that mattered to me. She began ripping her clothes off and of course, she didn't have panties on. She was bare naked underneath her skirt, which again, was a surprise as she always wore something underneath there.

After she got all of her clothes off, this time, she dropped down and began sucking my dick. As I said, foreplay wasn't something we did very often but when we did – the few times she actually sucked my dick – it was nothing like this. She was going to town on my cock, sucking it like she was sucking on the last popsicle left on earth.

The manner in which she was sucking it was like an art. Like a workout routine you see on one of those crazy fitness videos. It was like she was dancing and doing an exercise routine on my dick. But I am not complaining in the slightest. It felt amazing. In fact, it actually made me wonder why I did not like getting my dick sucked. Like I said, this particular technique she was doing to suck it was new, but still, it felt fucking amazing and made me realize everything I was missing out on in the past.

For the first time ever, it felt as if her lips were like the greatest thing that had ever touched my cock. The way she was sucking it, the speed she was sucking it, the motions she was doing while sucking it, it was all perfectly perfect. I wasn't sure exactly how long I could last. Twenty minutes was usually my limit, mind you, but what she was doing to my dick was a feeling I had never experienced before. It was intense and felt absolutely phenomenal. It felt so great, I swear no other woman or man or anything with lips could have sucked my dick half as good as she was currently doing at the moment.

All of a sudden, she pulled up with a big smile on her face. "You want me to fuck you?" She asked with slight horny tone.

"Of course!" I said in response. "Fuck me! I want you to! I want you to fuck me as good as you just sucked my dick!"

"How about I fuck you better than I sucked your dick!" She replied. "Hell yes!" I answered.

And then, she jumped up, spreading her legs wide and dropped down onto my dick and began to ride it like a cowgirl on cocaine. She was going fast and hard, faster and harder than she had ever done me before in the past. The swing began to bounce all around while swaying back and forth. It was almost like a musical beat and everything was in sync with one another.

She was riding my fucking dick like a champ. As I said, this was an entirely new side of her I had never seen before. Usually she's slow and gentle. Tonight, not so much. She was riding it like a crazy woman. Emphasis on crazy. Seriously, she was fucking wild!

She was staring me in the eye with an almost sinister look on her face. She was grinding her teeth together while breathing like a bull. She grabbed my shoulders and squeezed them as tightly as she could. Then, as she was bouncing up and down on my dick, she started doing that while simultaneously swaying her body side to side.

I started growing concerned that the swing was going to break as I could hear the hook hanging from the ceiling that it was connected to creaking. I looked up to examine it and all of a sudden, she slapped the living hell out of me. This was a shock as she had never done anything like that before nor did she ever act violent. But considering everything that had gone down today and the stunning turn of events and mind boggling revelations, this should actually be no surprise to me.

Right after she slapped me as hard as she could, she shouted, "Pay attention to me, pussy fucker! I'm in charge now! Not the fucking ceiling!"

"Yes, master!" I said as nicely as I possibly could say.

She kept bouncing up and down on my dick while swinging her body back and forth with her hands gripping my shoulders as tightly as they could. She began to make these deep, guttural grunting sounds. I honestly didn't know how to describe them as they were almost out of this world. She began to suck her stomach inward in a way that almost looked disgusting – like those people who can bend their arms in ways that the average ordinary person cannot – that kind of disgusting. Then, without warning, she jumped up and spun around – as we're still on the swing mind you – and spread her legs wide, then dropped down onto my dick in the reverse cowgirl position. Then, she picked back up where she left off, bouncing up and down on my dick. Now, her plump little ass was all I could see and it was a sight to behold. I loved her ass and loved looking at it from this angle. The swing just continued to rock and sway all around, making various squeaking and creaking noises, but stayed in place, surprisingly.

She kept on bouncing up and down, up and down, up and down, up and down and suddenly, I heard her cry out, "Stick your finger in my fucking asshole!"

"Did I hear her correctly?" I thought to myself. I had to take a moment to let that process because we never ever did anything anal nor did we ever talk about it. I mean, I know this was her coming out of the shell party, but seriously, what next? Does she really want me to stick my finger up her turd tunnel?

"I won't ask again!" She screamed. "Stick your fucking finger up my asshole! Now, dammit!" She commanded.

And so I tentatively took my finger and inched it closer and closer to her asshole that was bouncing up and down as she continued to ride my dick in the reverse cowgirl position. I had it pointed right at her ass when she said, "Stick it in now, dammit!

Right. Fucking. Now!"

And then, without hesitation, I just jabbed it right in her little ass hole. As soon as it entered, she squealed like a pig and I could tell she liked it. When it entered, it's like it turned her up a few more notches as well as she started riding me even harder and faster than before. I then began to fuck her ass with my finger as her screaming grew louder and a hell of a lot more intense.

Finally, after an hour passed, we found ourselves on the floor, wrapped up in each other's arms and covered in sweat. I had recently just came all inside of her mouth (and that was a first for us as a couple as well.).

At this point, I know we were passed the awkwardness but all I could think of was what would come next. What would the outcome of this be? Where would this new path we've ventured down lead us? We laid there in silence not saying a word. It's like one of those situations where you don't know what to say to the other. Similar to finding out something about someone and you don't want to say any-thing in fear of offending them. Yeah, it was like that and it was like that for not just me, but her as well.

And then, out of the blue, she dropped the hammer on me by saying, "I want you to watch me get fucked by another man."

Where the hell did that come from? Just when I thought she couldn't surprise me anymore, she sure as hell did!

"Why do you want that?" I asked. "Do you not love me or something?"

Then, she turned over looking at me and pleading with me in her eyes. I could tell she was desperate so I listened because she was that serious. She then said, "Of course I love you. I love you with all of my heart. And if you love me, you'll at least consider it. It's one of my fantasies and it turns me on. Believe me, I think it will turn you on as well. And just because I fuck another guy, doesn't mean I don't love you. I do. I'm just a sexual freak. What more can I say? But if you don't want to do it, then fine. We don't have to. I'll give you some time to think about it and just get back to me. Okay?"

I simply nodded in agreement. That was all I could do. And so, per her request, I went home and thought about her proposal. And by thinking about it, I don't mean thinking while I showered or brushed my teeth, I literally spent all night thinking about it and re-searching it. I researched testimonials from other cuckold boyfriends. They seemed to love it just as much as the wives and or girlfriends who were getting fucked did. And so, after long and careful consider-ation, I decided to honor her request by agreeing to do it. Sure, I was a wee bit skeptical, but at this point, it was worth a shot. After all, could it be any worse than finding out my girlfriend had a secret sex room? Of course not – at least in my opinion.

And so she made the arrangements and the time came for me to sit and watch as my girlfriend fucked another guy. The closer the date and time drew, the more eager and excited I got as I continued to watch cuckold porn and read stories and was actually growing more and more fond of it, getting really turned on by just the mere thought of it.

And so I made my way up to my girlfriend's apartments. It was time. I went in and was told to take a seat on the sex couch in the once secret sex room and so I did.

I sat and waited for roughly ten minutes and then all of a sudden, two already naked people came bursting through the door – it was my girlfriend and her lover – a tall, muscular bald guy with a dick that was borderline seven inches long.

He suddenly lifted her up, spread her legs and held her into the air as he ate her pussy out while she was in mid air like she was flying. She started screaming as her head jerked all over the place. Then he walked over to the couch, squatting down so that her face was angled directly in front of mine. He was licking that pussy raw as his face was moving side to side very fast as his tongue was hitting the g spot in her little pussy. Then he sat down right beside me and immediately dropped her down onto his cock. She began to bounce up and down on his long as dick – just as she was doing mine the other day. It was wild and crazy. His long as dick was stretching her tight little pussy open wide.

He looked over at me and said, "You like this? You like seeing your girlfriend get fucked by another man?"

And to be honest with you, I did. I wasn't sure what I was supposed to say or do here, but all I said was, "I sure do. Keep fucking her. Fuck her hard. Please fuck her hard."

"Oh I am! Isn't that right?" he said to me before looking to her and she just moaned in response, "Yeaaahhhhh! Ohhhh Yeaaaahhh!"

He then spun her around, stood up and held her in the air in the doggie style position as he stood there and began to pound her out from behind as she was held in mid air. It was an incredible sight to see! He started walking around the room, pounding her out from behind. As he walked by a particular long, black dildo, she reached over and shoved it into her mouth and began to suck it like she was really sucking a big black dick – all the while he continued ramming her pussy out from behind while holding her in mid air.

He then dropped her down onto the sex swing. They were still in the doggie style position but then he pushed the swing forward, causing his dick to come out. She flew forward and then back as his dick rung her little pussy hole. He started doing this going back and forth back and forth back and forth back and forth…

He then grew bored with it and held her still and then began ramming her from behind once again. He kept going and going and going at light speed. Then he grabbed that big black dildo out of her mouth and shoved it into her little asshole. Her face lit up like a light bulb in a pitch black dark room and she began to scream something I've never heard a human scream before. He was fucking her ass hard with that dildo simultaneously while he fucked her pussy hard and fast with his very own dick.

He then pulled his dick out but left the dildo in her asshole. He spun her around, picked her up as she wrapped her arms around his shoulders and legs around his waste. Then he put his dick in her and began to power fuck her while holding her in the air again. This guy was amazing! And that dildo didn't last but only a few thrusts before it fell out and hit the ground. He kicked it over to me and command-ed that I picked it up and smell it. Since I was the turned on cuckold bitch who was sitting here watching my girlfriend get fucked by him, I decided to answer his demands and do as he said. I picked that big black dildo up and smelled it and it smelled just like fresh female ass.

"Lick it! I said fucking lick it!" he commanded.

And so, I did just that. I began to lick that big black dildo clean. Surprisingly, it didn't taste bad. I kept licking it until all I could taste was the rubber of the dildo. I placed it down, sat back and watched as this stud muffing continued to fuck my once innocent and now freaky little girlfriend.

By now, he was on his back and she was on top of him in the sex swing and they were rocking back and forth as she rode him like a cowgirl. The swing itself kept ramming into the wall and all of the sex objects on the shelves connected to that very wall were falling off. That is how hard that swing was ramming into the wall.

He started flipping her around, moving, shaking, etc. as they were balled up in the swing, and it looked like two mice in a wool sock – literally. They were fucking like rabid wild animals in a wool sock. It was incredible and I was completely turned on and loving this. I couldn't help myself.

Then an arm reached out and grabbed a pair of anal beads that were on the ground. Then it disappeared back into the swing and all I could see was the swing moving as two bodies were fucking so wildly, it appeared as if they were wrestling. Then all I could hear was a squeal. Like something hit the spot. Next thing I know, another dildo came flying at me and all I heard was, "like that shit off!" "Yes, sir!" I answered as I grabbed that dildo and began to lick it clean once again – just as I did the last one.

Eventually, they were fucking so hard, the swing actually broke and they both fell to the ground. But crazily enough, that didn't stop them. They kept fucking hard and wild without even pausing. It's as if they didn't even know the swing had broken.

Finally, they broke out of the swing and he had her lifted into the air again, fucking her doggie style while holding her mid air. This was insane to say the least.

While carrying her, he rammed her into the walls, knocking what was left of the sex toys off the shelves – the ones that weren't on the floor already. They were circling the room while fucking simultaneously. It was so loud and rocking, I simply could not believe the neighbors weren't hearing it. I just expected any second now we would receive a knock at the front door and I would have to be the one to go and answer it. But no! Everything continued as normal – well at least in terms of not being bothered by outsiders. I honestly couldn't believe they weren't knocking holes in the wall either because he was ramming her into the walls pretty hard. Yet, no dents, holes, nothing!

Another hour passed and they were on the couch and she was sucking his dick. He had his legs spread wide open beside me. I could see his balls and dark little asshole. He was moaning and groaning as she was sucking his dick hard. Finally, he blew a load into her mouth and she swallowed every bit of it. She looked at me, smiling with that guy's very own cum glued to her teeth. She started acting shy – which was ironic and a tad bit strange. The guy never said a word. He just laid there trying to catch his breath. I of course enjoyed the show and was very turned on by it. In fact, I was ready to jump in on the action but there was no way I would do it in front of this manly machine because I could never top him in a million years or a million tries.

So she looked at me with a glow in her eyes and said, "What do you think, babe?" I simply smiled and said, "I think I'm ready for an encore…"

And she looked to her lover as he leaned his head up. Then, she swallowed what was left of his cum in her mouth, hopped on top of his dick, spread her legs wide open and swallowed his dick completely with her pussy as round two began…